DOG WATCHES

—

DOG WATCHES

STORIES FROM THE SEA

ROLF YNGVE

SADDLE ROAD PRESS

Dog Watches
© 2018 Rolf Yngve

Saddle Road Press
Hilo, Hawai'i
saddleroadpress.com

Cover and book design by Don Mitchell
The cover image was developed from an official photograph of a destroyer retrieving a lifeboat after a hostage rescue. The original is a U.S. Marine Corps photo by Lance Cpl. Megan E. Sindelar, USMC, released and distributed by the US Navy Visual News Service.

Dog Watches is a work of fiction. No events, persons, or units depicted here are real, and no inference should be made to actual events.

ISBN 978-0-9969074-9-1
Library of Congress Control Number: 2018909365

"A Prerogative" appeared in *Kenyon Review*; "Michael E. Austin, Arriving" in *Review Americana* (online under a different title); "Efendim" in *Indiana Review*; "Billy" in *Eclipse*; "Personal Effects" in *Chattahoochee Review*; "The Mouse" in *War, Literature and the Arts Journal* (online) and "Pointed Fair" in *Proud to Be: Writing by American Warriors Vol 2*.

v1.1

For Sharon

CONTENTS

A shortened watch is called a dog.

A Prerogative

He was not an unhappy man. It had been an easy morning commute, the Pacific air rinsed clean by an early rain. A cheerful few hours at his desk, all good news, even the stock market up, and his day had moved peacefully along through a clear spring afternoon. A canceled appointment, no more meetings. Why lean over the flat screen, read email when he had been so obviously beckoned to obey the impulse? Leave early. Get out of the office! This age in life, he had earned the right to exercise a little prerogative, and damned if he would give it up to satisfy a civilian job where nothing mattered except someone else's bottom line. Screw'em—take that quick slide home. See if you can get the roses trimmed. His wife would be pleased.

But nothing is ever that easy. On the ramp up to the bay bridge, traffic muscled in and slowed him to a walk. Probably a stalled vehicle. Maybe one of those drivers who find themselves too alarmed to continue, so high above water.

He tried to sidestep his old Corolla into the clear lane, but a truck the size of a landing craft pinned him in. He thought, life in the slow lane. Jim Ehrlich trapped in the fucking slow lane. Of all the luck.

He had to stop.

Twenty feet ahead, a woman stood behind a deep green vehicle at the edge of the bridge, a Jeep, jammed into a concrete barrier. A fender bender. Nothing more. Ehrlich thought, this sort of thing happens. People know what to do. He put on his turn signal, hoping someone would let him get going again. A silver Mercedes slowed, flashed its lights. He could have rolled on over the bridge to the island and home. But he put the Corolla in park, set the brake. He would never know why.

She was a young woman with short, blond hair cut high over the nape of her neck, her hands jammed into the pockets of a dark blue jacket too light to keep anyone warm. Tight black jeans, her waist at the top of the concrete barrier between her and a fall. She looked down toward the water.

Ehrlich killed the car, took his keys. A pretty girl. Early twenties or younger. A semi-truck in low gear struggled past them. The bridge trembled. She leaned forward, placed her hands palms down, then her foot flat on the top of the barrier. A dancer's move.

"Hey! Hey, wait!"

Her shoulders jerked. Her foot twisted and slipped off. She folded down into a half curl, then straightened, stared at him. "*Stay the fuck away from me, Fucker.*"

"Sure," said Ehrlich. "No sweat."

The roadway was littered with bits of plastic, sheared steel, glass. The scent of oil. Tar. She had smooth, browned California skin. Her cheeks were wet. When people this young worked for him in the Navy, Ehrlich had always kept a box of Kleenex on his desk.

"Here." Ehrlich fumbled in his pocket. "I've got a handkerchief. Take it."

The girl turned to face him. Big, narrow-set eyes, a piece of glitter on her nose. She said something angry, but he missed it in the rattle of a passing car with a bad muffler. Maybe it *was* only an accident. Someone in the opposite lane leaned on a horn. She wiped her nose on the arm of the thin jacket, slipped herself up to sit on top of the barrier, another graceful move. She turned her blank face to the road. Closed her eyes. Then, ever so slowly, she seemed to lean backward.

"No. Wait. You don't understand…"

She froze, mumbled something. He reached down into his chest for his command voice. "Listen. Get down off that wall. Now." He started to move toward her, his hand out, the handkerchief clenched in a fist.

She jerked herself upright, thrashed the air with her arms, her eyes squeezed shut, face twisted into an awful grin. "Just—just go AWAY! Don't you come any closer. Oh." Her voice was broken and wet. She had been crying for a while.

Ehrlich straightened his back. He took a long breath.

"Easy now. No need to do this."

"What do you know?"

What *did* he know? Maybe she had a right, her prerogative, but he couldn't leave, and he couldn't bear the idea of seeing her fall. Hot on the bridge, now. No wind. Maybe he could saunter up to the barrier, get close enough to grab her. The bright sun lowered toward the sea beyond the island. There was no shade. Light poles stretched up on either side of the roadway and above, a vertigo sky, and he thought, why not?

"Look," he said. "I'll do it for you."

She sniffed, wiped her nose on her jacket sleeve again. "What?"

"Don't you want the handkerchief? No?" Ehrlich stuffed it into the pocket of his suit coat.

The girl said, "What are you?" She sounded angry, now. "I told you. Leave me alone."

Ehrlich held up his hand. "Just give me a minute." He took off his suitcoat, untangled his tie and found his hands full. Fuck it, he thought, fuck all of it. He thought about throwing the suit coat over the edge into the air, but there was a net of heavy cable below the bottom edge of the bridge. He dropped them both on the concrete roadway. The company's classified phone in his pocket smacked the pavement. Broke it, for sure. He would have to pay somebody back for that one.

Then it occurred to him, he didn't have to care about a broken cell-phone, did he? It was a strange sort of freedom, imagining for a moment he wouldn't have to worry about filling out the form, the pittance it would cost to replace that gear. He said to her, to himself, to the air, "Damn. I wasn't ready for this."

The girl said, "For what? You're going to do what? Jump?" She was sneering at him, but she wasn't crying anymore. Good, he thought. They never pay attention until they've finished crying.

"That's right. I said, you don't have to do it. I will instead."

Ehrlich set his hands gently onto the top of the barrier. Very warm. Almost hot. A melted plastic scent like new, raw paint on a ship's deck. Below and far out, a cluster of sailboats crept upwind on the sparkling bay. Ashore, people had gathered. Low tide. Were they watching? Did they know?

He could still drive away, join them. He could look back, see the bridge, its elegant legs under that graceful curve between the island and shore.

She stepped down off the barrier onto the roadway. She seemed to weigh nothing, so delicate. She trailed her fingertip along the top of the concrete as she took one, then another step toward him. "What are you talking about?"

"Look at that." He pointed down. The girl twisted herself around. Three small boats had arranged themselves in a triangle beneath them. They loitered in the shadow of the bridge, the water nearly black. Ehrlich told her, "Cops. Two harbor patrol and one coast guard. They need the coast guard in case someone jumps onto federal property."

"Federal what?"

"The shipyard." At the foot of the bridge, a warship stood high up out of the water. White plastic tarps covered its masts and equipment littered the decks. A crowd had gathered on the bow.

"That's a destroyer. Federal property. I had command of a ship like that once. Not in command of anything now. Maybe in command of my senses—look. Why were you? Why were you going to do it? I mean. I got a right to know."

He leaned forward on the barrier, held himself away from the concrete to keep his suit pants from the grime.

She whispered something too quietly to hear.

More people were coming out of the destroyer's superstructure. Ehrlich said, "Jeez. We got quite an audience down there. I guess you don't need a reason, do you?"

He hoisted himself up onto the barrier, swung one leg over. He had kept himself pretty much in shape. "I mean, you've got a point. Why not?" He brought the other leg around, stepped down outside the barrier. The wire safety netting had been beautifully made, splendid workmanship.

"This is such bullshit. Creep. Asshole." The girl was on the other side of the barrier before he could say anything. But she wasn't in danger. She stood on the heavy cables. All his life he had inspected safety nets like this on the flight decks of his ships. This one was clean steel, not a speck of rust. She reached back, held herself to the bridge.

Ehrlich told her, "Go on. Get back on the other side."

"Fuck you." She had the clearest brown eyes. "You won't jump."

A little breeze floated up to them. "I ripped my pants." Ehrlich reached down, twisted around, examined the open slit on the seam. Light summer wool, good for nothing except sitting around. "Maybe I should have kept my jacket on?"

Now she looked alarmed.

"Sorry. I don't want to…"

"What?"

"Upset you. Here. Here. Take this." He fumbled his beefy wallet out of his back pocket, held it up. "No? No? Then get it later, ok? Take anything in it." He flipped the billfold onto the bridge. All the credit cards, business cards, loose ID, spilled out in a clutter.

"Mister. *Sir.* Don't."

Now she cared? Did it make any difference to him whether or not she cared? Would they put something in the papers? Would those people watching from the ship know this was another one of those old ex-Navy assholes, not even full of regret, just tired? Empty. He didn't remember anything about the bridge jumpers in the papers or on the news. No names. Always pending notification of the next of kin. Never a follow-up he could remember, all those jumpers still pending. Strange, he thought, no traffic. The cops must have stopped it. They would be here soon enough. He fished around in his pocket. "Here. Take these. Here's the keys. You can't have the car, I guess. Give the keys to the cops, will you?"

"I don't want anything."

"No? Sure you do. You want something." He let the keys drop. They clicked against the cable, slipped out of sight too fast then fell much longer than he thought possible. One of the boats lurched up to speed, curved toward the place where his keys had hit the water.

"That's why they have the boats, I guess. Sometimes people survive the fall. Nobody wants to let them drown." Could he live through it? It was out of his hands. What difference would it make to hope? You don't have to even hope anymore. It occurred to him that he could get her to jump with him if he wanted to do so. That would make the papers for sure.

It occurred to him he should tell her, "Look, you don't want to do something like this because you're mad at somebody or feeling sorry for yourself." Far away and below, he heard the shrill peel of a boatswain's pipe, then unintelligent words from a loudspeaker. The people on the bow of the destroyer started to leave. "Good on him, that captain. Did you hear that? He made his crew go back inside. They don't need to see this sort of thing."

"I believe you. Now. I believe you. But I'm going to jump anyway."

"No. You're not."

Ehrlich lowered himself to his knees onto the wire. Lousy pants. He wished he had on his uniform trousers. A little crawling around on a safety net wouldn't rip those old washed khakis. "It isn't safe to try to walk out on these nets. You gotta take care or you'll slip through and break your leg or your nuts. Sorry. I didn't mean to say something vulgar."

"If you think you're making me feel any better…"

He didn't bother to look at her. "This has nothing to do with making anyone feel better. I said I'd do it for you. So. Don't you want to know my name? No? That's ok. What's yours?"

He glanced over his shoulder at her. Her right knee quivered. She said, "Casey. My name's Casey."

"Good. Casey. I bet you have a tattoo. You know that's a weird thing, thirty-five years in the Navy, I never got a tattoo. Always thought it would set a bad example. Christ." He had reached the edge. The netting seemed insubstantial, but he knew that was nonsense. The cables were heavy enough. But the drop. The empty drop. "Oh. This is scary. You know, really scary. I wonder—are people too scared to keep their eyes open, or too scared to close them?"

"Don't you have a wife? Kids or something? Come back here, ok? I promise I won't. We can leave? You and me? Please?"

Ehrlich swiveled himself to face her, sat cross-legged. "Dumb. A tattoo. I wish I'd gotten—did it hurt? Getting your tattoo? Did you have to get drunk first?" The girl had clamped both arms over the top of the barrier.

Now she was afraid.

Now she was safe.

He tried to stand, almost lost his balance, then he was upright and alone with that obscene silence. A peaceful breeze filled in the surface of the sun-spattered bay, the air sweet, smooth and awful. The clear sight down to the island beyond where people can see the bridge reflected on the shore's wetter ground.

Ehrlich looked out to a lean horizon. A destroyer raising its hull had made the channel turn standing her into port. Such warships always seem so calm at a distance, the day gone, gun laid to rest, the decks stowed fore and aft, all lines rigged. The ends of such days, so much comfort from routine passage-making with the sun astern casting its light deep into the harbor, and he was there, in the pilothouse, the watch still keeping all at ease—helmsman and lookout, officer of the deck and messenger, navigator and he, himself, their captain, in command to bring this ship to its mooring, this ship he had been given. To deliver all the crew he served safely home.

The girl said, "Please. You don't have to do this."

"Sure." Ehrlich nodded, tapped his temple with a forefinger, pointed at her. He said, "You don't have to see it."

Michael E. Austin, Arriving

One night while encamped near Da Nang, the Republic of South Vietnam, Navy Corpsman First Class Michael E. Austin found himself next to a live Chinese grenade after a major league pitch into his sandbag parapet by a Viet Cong—which was unusual because most of the Viet Cong had been wiped out during the Tet Offensive three years earlier. Company A, 1ˢᵗ Battalion, 3rd Marines had gotten used to having Austin as their medic and three Marines in his platoon had decided to teach him how to play pinochle. No one expected a gook to heave a grenade all the way over the sandbags from outside the wire. But there it was, in the mud, sputtering. Petty Officer Austin, as related in his citation, "in complete disregard for his own safety" then did throw himself upon the grenade and "smothered the explosion with his own body." In so doing, Petty Officer Austin saved the three Marines and earned the decoration known as the Navy Cross.

One would think that such sacrifice always results in an extraordinary decoration, especially posthumously. But the truth is, such recognition does not come to pass without the fortune to have had a witness to write a citation. In this case, a Marine Corps sergeant gave the facts to his platoon commander, a second lieutenant who would lose three fingers on his left hand and sight in one eye before he could write any sort of citation.

The sergeant, however, was persistent. Knowing that Austin's selfless act would be lost in the usual exhaustion, ennui and paperwork that comes after engagement with the enemy, he brought the circumstances forward to his acting company commander, a captain who would complete a tour in Vietnam and a thirty-year career in politics mostly intact in part due to the fact that he knew how to write with clarity and conviction. The captain actually recommended Petty Officer Austin for the nation's highest decoration, the Medal of Honor, which is sometimes given to those who smother grenades with their own bodies when such activity is considered "above and beyond the call of duty." But the recommendation was downgraded to the Navy Cross owing to the battalion reviewing officer's observation that no commissioned officer had actually witnessed the act and the incident had not occurred while Petty Officer Austin was actively attending to wounded and dying Marines. Rather, he had been sitting around shooting the shit and playing cards and, as such, he had merely "distinguished himself or herself in action by extraordinary heroism in combat...", but not enough to be above and beyond the call of duty.

Downgraded as such, USS *Michael E. Austin* would never have been christened in honor of the dead sailor if not for the fact that a particular Secretary of the Navy had personal knowledge of Michael E. Austin's performance. This SECNAV, as he is known, exercised his right as the senior civilian leader of the United States Navy and, instead of naming a destroyer after a dead admiral or a politician, cited the corpsman from his unit who had paid the ultimate price.

The former sergeant had not been surprised to hear that the award he'd proposed for Petty Office Austin had been downgraded to the Navy Cross, but he was also not disappointed. In fact, he had presumed that nothing at all had come from the recommendation because he'd never heard anything about the award until his former captain company commander, now SECNAV, located him at his home in Eden Prairie, Minnesota and was not only able to inform him that his recommendation had been at least partially successful, but invite him to the commissioning of USS *Michael E. Austin*.

At first, the former sergeant thought he would decline the invitation. While the sergeant had found a successful life for himself, it was nothing like the stratosphere of this Secretary of the Navy who he had barely known and had never particularly liked for no reason other than he was an officer who had not been around long enough to register in his company's memory. Furthermore, the former sergeant had spent too many nighttime hours turning over and over in his bed-sheets, twisting around the notion that Petty Officer Austin had erred.

When the grenade slapped into the mud at their feet, the sergeant and the other Marines had run a couple of steps, then scrambled over the sandbags where they waited heartbeats before Petty Officer Austin found himself scattered across the canvas and dirt walls of the parapet. (All of this "smothering the explosion with his own body" is a bit coy. *Scattered* gives the more accurate depiction of human detritus flung haphazard about the walls of a ditch.) What the sergeant knew, Michael E. Austin had dumped his helmet on the grenade, fallen on top, clutched it to his belly and tried to squirm his nuts out of the way while he waited for it to go off. A long wait while the sergeant and the other members of the squad had cowered down out of sight in the fear and knowledge of what was about to happen to Austin. Then, they had cowered in the hope that it had been a dud after all. Then, they had cowered in the horror that it had not.

The sergeant had not seen the detonation, only witnessed the outcome, one of several particularly disturbing memories he first nurtured, then overcame and finally set aside to become a splendid husband and father, even though he had never quit wondering, why Austin? Why not me? He would wrestle late into the night, all the while knowing the answer; Austin had been the one who jumped on the grenade, that simple. Austin had been the one with all the questions answered.

But there were errors.

What he had done and what he had failed to do—his own error—was the memory the former sergeant visited as he sat in the padded, folding chair of the front row during the commissioning ceremony of the ship named after his comrade-in-arms. With two hundred fifteen other guests, he watched USS Michael E. Austin brought alive through the crew's collective leap up the gangway to take their positions at the lifelines as the signal flags and the national ensign broke open on halyards, all arrayed in lively color above what had been merely a dull, grey hull with a number on the bow. Finally, the new captain of the new ship strode forward as cocky as any bantam. Two sharp strokes of the ship's bell, then two more pealed from the ship's loudspeaker and all across the audience, the pier, the naval station itself the words echoed: Michael E. Austin, Arriving!

The former sergeant watched the ship's first commanding officer salute the national ensign, then step aboard to one more smart, single stroke on the bell, signifying the placement of his foot upon the hull of the ship whose name he would bear while in command, the name of the corpsman the former sergeant had failed to protect.

Of course, the former sergeant felt grateful to have lived through the war to earn his honorable discharge. He was grateful for his career appraising real estate, and even more grateful for the family he had found despite the ever-more-sure knowledge he could have grabbed Austin by the scruff of the neck, snagged him, hauled him up over the sandbags and out of the way of what should have been a useless grenade. Now, grown and believing he would one day abandon that memory forever, he had been obligated to see the ship bearing the name Michael E. Austin go into commission while he sat next to a slim woman in a neat blue suit who seemed composed, even radiant. It had been nearly fifteen years since she lost her middle son to that Chinese hand grenade, and she did not seem bitter about anything at all. She told her son's sergeant that she had committed him to the Lord.

Unreasonably, the former sergeant found this offensive. He had never met Austin's mother before, and he supposed he should be glad to see her so proud of her son, a hero. But he could not leave the conviction that the man who had fallen on that grenade had not been as much a hero as he had been another victim who had glanced up at him, the sergeant, and perhaps, Him, with eyes that may have been full of hope and forgiveness. Or perhaps, accusation. Perhaps anger. But most certainly full of the question, why me?

The sergeant thought his mother should be asking, why him? Why did this have to happen to my child? Why me? Why did he have to be the one committed to the Lord?

The sergeant thought, if she only knew how terrible it had been to see her son torn to a pulp, his eyes still wondering, why me?

And hadn't Petty Officer Austin dropped that helmet on top of the grenade in the weird hope that perhaps he might be spared? Forgiven? Saved? Had he imaged he might even able to receive the Navy Cross in person, a chunk of bronze dangled under its pristine blue and white ribbon? Was his faith the sort of illusion that his sergeant, now sitting next to his mother, might have the power to spare him in some way?

Austin had not died immediately. He had been given enough time to whisper those things they whisper and the former sergeant had been privileged enough to hear Petty Officer Austin call for God, then his mother who now sat next to the former sergeant who would always, always remain Petty Officer Austin's sergeant—two of them hearing and watching her son's namesake ship brought into being, the sparkling voice, the clean hull spanking new under the sun that rippled across the flags of that morning, hearing those bells stroked two by two in about the same cadence as the time it took for that grenade to go off.

Did the former sergeant take some solace from his sure knowledge that whoever may command this ship, for as long as they command, shall have their arrival or departure aboard any warship heralded with four strokes on the bell, two shrill heartbeats, and the name of an honored Navy Corpsman, a hero, pealed out: *Michael E. Austin,* and his state of being: *Arriving, Returning, Departing?* Would we—those of us who will live aboard this ship, crew it, break it, repair it, fight it—would we believe this to be some sort of atonement, this announcement of the name of a dead man every arrival or departure of our captain?

Some will.

Most won't.

In the end, ship's names are announced only to pass a bit of information to the crews of naval vessels. The bells say: the commanding officer of a naval vessel in commission with all its potency, history and skills has arrived on board. The broadcast of the ship's name signifies only a commanding officer's transit between one place of command to another, another routine moment of the many that fill a ship's short life.

Every arrival and departure, all of the crew of Michael E. Austin will evermore hear the bells rung, two-by-two, *Michael E. Austin, Returning!* He is Michael E. Austin. We who serve aboard *USS Michael E. Austin* will think nothing of the flesh and blood Michael E. Austin other than the faded black and white picture of a skinny boy in a dress uniform affixed above his citation to be read by newcomers and visitors to the crew's mess of the ship named after him.

Michael E. Austin, Arriving. Michael E. Austin, Departing.

The Dog Watch

The dog watch after the evening meal is one of very few quiet moments for a strike group commander at sea. Everyone else, all five thousand sailors and officers on the vast aircraft carrier with its squadrons, staffs, divisions and detachments, spends that hour flailing through the daily reports, written, then reviewed, rewritten and approved at various levels in the chains of command. Finally, the reports will be distilled into the evening flag briefing when the strike group commander will spend an hour at the long table in her conference room listening to the ship's captain, the air wing commander, and the officers on her staff serve up all the news of the day: the sorties flown, missions engaged, orders given, milestones reached. Her night orders will be written for her, then rewritten and she will sign them. She will approve the airwing's air plan for tomorrow and review the operational orders received from fleet commanders and commanders in chief. She will be busy until well into the first night watch as she has been since dawn. But for an hour at the end of the dog watch, everyone else is too busy to bother her.

Strangely, she cannot seem to take advantage of what should be stolen time alone to write a letter, read a book, email her husband, search out any of those connections to normal life ashore. Perhaps it is the habit born out of all the dog watches of her career that calls her to the watch floor where the current operations team has learned to expect hearing her squeak into her chair next to the FWO, the Flag Watch Officer. The four sailors bent over their computer screens and cathode ray tubes appreciate consistency, procedure, normal events, even in the midst of an operation like this one and they are comforted by her routine presence in the dark, cool cavern of information they occupy. They nod in recognition when they hear her ask the FWO her usual brand of question as if nothing important was happening, "Whaddaya think of those Yankees?" They like the fact that the FWO usually gets a little less obnoxious when she's on deck, and they like it best when this particular FWO is on watch. He's a Marine, an unusual assignment as an FWO on a fleet staff, and maybe being a Marine on her staff is the reason he seems so relaxed. He's not in any sort of competition with the other officers; no one expects him to be promoted. A lieutenant colonel now, he has been on the staff nearly three years, too long for a Marine Aviator to be out of the cockpit. As for the boss, she likes the way Butch ignores her question about the Yankees and says: "You worried, Admiral? About Oscar?"

"You mean, USS Michael E. Austin?"

The command center is quiet. The watch has also been worried about Oscar. The ventilation sighs its chilling air over the electronics. Touch the insulation over the steel bulkheads walls and you can feel the heat and sense the dust hovering over the Arabian Sea. Take a deep breath and you can detect the faint electric conduction through the cables and wires crisscrossed under the drop ceiling and raised deck. CNN murmurs from one of the small displays hovering above the collection of computer terminals where the watch has displayed all the information for the USS *Michael E. Austin* enroute her mission. Alone. No allied unit within four hundred miles. Sent to rescue a hostage. The watch is tuned to their tasks, ears encased in their headsets, their chat rooms ready, their internal communications set, their web pages organized. All they can do is wait, and at every watch station, one ear peaks out from under the headset to hear what their admiral will say.

"No, Butch. Not worried about them. Why do you ask?"

The FWO thinks he probably pushed the envelope a little far with this sort of question. He gets away with a little of that Marine Corps bluntness, but he considers his next statement more carefully, "Current ops got a bunch of questions about *Austin* from the staff after your morning brief. Someone said you had a lot of questions."

"Yes. I suppose I did." The admiral leans back in her chair. They had managed to make pretty good coffee. Not the bitter, oily stuff she'd learned to tolerate thirty years ago on her first ship. She was going to leave it at that; you have to let Marines be Marines. That's why you want officers like Butch around you. To keep you straight. But perhaps her belief this would be her last duty station, perhaps being the first woman to command a strike group, perhaps the need to pass the time made her think, why not? Why not tell him about this ship? She took a sip from her cup. Not bitter at all. And hadn't every ship been her last?

"What do you know about *Michael E. Austin*, Butch?"

"Well, not much, Admiral. She's a destroyer. We're going to have to refuel her sometime in the next three days. Wish she had more fuel. We got the SEALs out to her. She was the only ship we had at the time."

Butch wonders, what is the admiral angling for? Maybe the mission. The Marine in him makes him decide to mimic a line the admiral often uses. "She'll either rescue the hostage, or not. She'll either come through, or not."

The strike group commander gave him a little smile. "Reputation. I mean, units get a reputation in the Marine Corps. The squadrons you flew with had reputations. I'm right?"

"Yes ma'am. Everybody knows who's who."

"And a ship like *Michael E. Austin* gets a reputation. Maybe it will change over time, but it's always there. So take old *Oscar*. A ship like that, you could call her the *Might Mike*. Or the *Awesome Austin*. Or anything at all. But they've called her *Oscar* for twenty years."

"Oscar." Butch punched a button on his console and hooked the symbol for USS *Michael E. Austin*, less than twenty miles from a broken-down lifeboat with a hostage on board. He expected that to be the end of it. Now the admiral would get up, say something funny for the watch, and be off to her dinner.

Instead, she leaned back into her chair, and says, "So there was a mustang. A real mustang, not some NROTC grad but a bonafide enlisted boot seaman who goes all the way up through the ranks to officer, then up again until he gets command. And he's got this four-star-admiral pal. He'd been a chief petty officer on the guy's ship. This admiral weighs in on the selection board so he gets the job as the first commanding officer of USS *Michael E. Austin*. Everybody knows this guy. He's an old officer of the old kind who brings a pit bull on a leash to the ship and keeps a gun room in his basement at home. He's the guy who gets the nod for the prize ship in the fleet. Brand new—he's risen high enough to command, and for some reason I'll never understand, he decides to carry out a man overboard drill one afternoon by jumping over the side."

"He what?"

"I'll give the old boy this much, he had the good sense to take a life jacket with him."

"A man overboard drill?

A sunny, warm summer day off the coast of San Diego in a calm sea, the after lookout heard someone hollering, "Hey, hey—you! After lookout!" He snapped himself awake from his half doze and found himself astonished to see his commanding officer hatless, his thinning grey hair as mussed up as bedsheets. He looked around for some help, a chief, a petty officer maybe, even his leading seaman, but he was alone on the fantail with his commanding officer.

"Yes. You. Is there some other after lookout? Man overboard! Make your report! Man overboard!" His captain was dancing himself into one of the huge kapok lifejackets the after lookout and his fellow seamen wore on deck for hazardous evolutions. He watched the captain fumble the straps between his legs, snug them up either side of his balls and boom out, "Well? Dammit! Your report?"

The after lookout felt his knees go watery. He eked out, "Aye aye, sir!" and pressed the button down on the mouthpiece of the sound powered phones, too hot over his ears, the black fabric still damp from the lookout he'd relieved, the rubber mouthpiece stinking in the sun. With the loud, clear voice he'd been trained to use, he made this report: "Bridge—After lookout. Man overboard, man OVER board, man overboard!" and was instantly queried, "Williams. You screwed up the report already. Which side?"

He had indeed screwed up the report and the captain, the man in front of him, demanded absolute perfection. His omission alone would cause the captain to fail a drill, which is where he thought he existed, in the make-believe universe of a drill. Is it any wonder that his voice sounded less than firm when he called out, "Which side, Captain?"

"Guess!" The captain had his back to him walking toward the starboard lifelines. He turned, waved, tried to swing his leg up over the top lifeline, but it looked as though he was too stiff. He stepped up on the lowest lifeline, made it over the top, and disappeared.

In boot camp, seamen learn the basic elements of their trade from *The Blue Jacket's Manual*. No one is called a blue jacket in the Navy anymore, but the name of the manual persists and much of the original advice is preserved intact from the days before airplanes, telephones, and decent refrigeration. It begins: "Shipmates, the book you're about to read is a resource that will last you the rest of your careers in our great NAVY." It tells the shipmates, "When someone goes overboard, prompt action is essential."

Clear enough direction for the after lookout and he remembered the words.

But *The Blue Jacket's Manual* is limited as are all manuals. While the concept of prompt action is critical, it does not discuss the contingency of the captain going overboard and for an instant, the after lookout thought this might be the captain's prerogative, to jump over the side. He though perhaps he shouldn't report it. After all, if the captain did it, wasn't it all right? Besides, no one liked the captain that much or the horrible pit bull he liked to have in his stateroom when they were in port. For a moment, he considered keeping the captain's departure a secret. And besides, it was a clear calm day. Someone would see him soon enough. Maybe.

Then, he had a terrible thought. It could only mean one thing—the captain must have jumped in to save the man overboard. His split second of confusion relieved, the after lookout knew what to report as he yelled into the soft rubber of the sound powered microphone, "Starboard side. Man overboard, Starboard Side. The commanding officer has jumped in after him! The CO is trying to rescue him! He's in the water. *Man overboard!*" He threw a life ring in the water as he had been taught. He pointed to the one dark spot he could see on the calm water as he'd been taught, a head bobbing as *USS Michael E. Austin* executed a smart turn to rescue the man overboard and retrieve the captain.

The true origin of the captain's notion to jump over the side came from a story the captain's father had told him about a CO on a tin-can destroyer in the old 1950's Navy when CO's took a little initiative and ran by-God US Naval Vessel like by-fucking-God-men, "That old son of a bitch, he'd jump over the side to test out the man overboard drill. Wild-ass," his former chief petty officer father had said with awe. "Absolute, crazy wild-ass. Not much appreciated by the officers, but the crew loved him."

Is it any wonder, then, that the son of that chief petty officer would harbor such a notion to himself, without an utterance, that one day, if ever he ascended to command, he would test his ship like those captains of yore? He had nurtured this thought through pay-grade after pay-grade promotion up to chief petty officer, then his amazing selection at the very top end of the age waiver for commissioning as a regular officer, then years at sea until he found himself detailed to USS *Michael E. Austin* as the first officer in command, the man who makes the ship's reputation.

And this is the point: he would have brought *Michael E. Austin* on her first deployment—new, every pump, motor and radar spanking new and wrung out, perfect working order, freed of time's wearing entropy, freed of accumulated error. He had been hand-picked to bring USS *Michael E. Austin* into the light with every nut and bolt tightened and leading a special crew, those first assigned to any ship, the *Plank Owners*. These are the crew who make a destroyer come alive clean and correct and now, finally, twenty years after the fact, Plank Owners long out of service watch TV, check the internet, and listen to the radio blaring the name USS *Michael E. Austin*, their ship, and begin to overcome that humiliating moment when their captain decided to step off the transom instead of into the promotion and career he thought he'd already earned.

He could have done. He, this former chief petty officer and son of a chief petty officer, could have found himself promoted to admiral. Who knows? Such things can happen. But he had been in the habit of dragging Oscar, the man overboard dummy, out of his cabin at odd hours and flinging the bright orange mannequin with its crazy grin into the water to test the lookout's alertness, the ship's response, and exercise the retrieval of a man overboard as all ships must regularly do. He graded the ship on every single detail of the recovery. The quick reaction of the lookouts. The immediate heaving of a life-ring in the water. The speedy launch of a rescue boat. The sounding of five short blasts of the whistle to alert ships nearby and the hoisting of the universal signal for man overboard, for every sailor's nightmare, being lost at sea—the signal flag used to represent the letter O—flag Oscar.

There is no pleasure like command of an extremely fit ship that responds with lightning efficiency to any test, always alert, always sound, always quietly professional. It creates a sort of euphoria where the commanding officer feels as though the ship is an extension of some broad, ordered universe and he, in command, is somehow both servant and slave to this extraordinary clockwork of order. The impulse to test it further, push the boundary becomes almost irresistible for some in command. Drill is only good if it is drilled and this first commanding officer of USS Michael E. Austin had been mightily pleased with the alacrity and efficiency of these drills. But he could not escape searching for the soul of the ship he wanted where he would be *not much appreciated by the officers, but the crew loved him.*

Perhaps that's what made him abandon Oscar, jump over the side himself. Out of love. Out of the desire to be loved.

Man overboard. Throw the life ring. Launch the boat. Sound the whistle. Hoist the flag, Oscar. Pray.

The XO of USS Michael E. Austin was the first one to realize there had been no one else in the water. All the bridge watch discovered a sudden emptiness in the pits of their stomachs and chest when the rescue boat wheeled back to the ship after recovering the captain and everyone realized they were not continuing to search for anyone else. They dreaded what would happen next, and wondered at the name of the dead crewmember, then found themselves astonished when the captain scampered into the pilothouse, had the boatswain pipe "all hands" under the still terrified eyes of the officer of the deck who had imagined he would be forever known as the officer of the deck who let his captain drown along with whoever else had disappeared.

The XO held the results of an incredibly quick muster of all the crew a muster that had shown no one missing except— the captain. The XO was the only one not surprised when the rescued, dripping wet, elated commanding officer delivered the short, invigorating, morale-boosting speech he'd been planning his entire life. USS *Michael E. Austin*, hearing how well they had done, responded with equal joy, that outpouring of love and respect all good ships keep in reserve for those very best officers, those wild-assed, superb officers who inspired all within their view.

The captain in a fit of humor the entire crew shared, had the boatswain's mate of the watch tap the bell, two strokes then two more, and announce, "*Michael E. Austin, Returning!*"

The strike group commander looks up to the drop ceiling tiles hiding all the snares of wire and cable conveying the tactical and operational picture of the Arabian Gulf and the Indian Ocean to the watch stationed in front of their computer screens, all of them aching to hear every word. She stops to consider, knows this is a moment when what she says will echo forward, and perhaps even back, into time.

"Who knows what makes us do the things we do? Instinct? Brain fart? Everyone called him 'Oscar' until the day he left the service. Imagine what his crew thought. Imagine the ship's XO when the old man brought them back into port."

The FWO watches his strike group commander lean forward to stare at the screen, and knows the admiral doesn't see anything, isn't hearing any report, isn't even there in that room.

"You were the XO, weren't you, Admiral?"

"I thought someone must have pushed him over the side. Plenty of people didn't much like him. But who would have done it? Maybe some sociopath. I thought it might be a strange suicide attempt, some PTSD thing. You know. The sort of thing that makes a guy like him have three or four wives and keep a pit bull and a gun room to show off to visitors. Sometimes people disappear. One hour you get a muster on them and they are keeping their watch, the next muster, gone. Sometimes. But this? No. I couldn't believe it."

They had spent another night at sea, and the XO of USS *Michael E. Austin* who would one day become the first woman to command a strike group spent it contemplating the end of her career. She stayed awake past midnight, saw the midwatch onto station, and finally settled onto the amazingly comfortable foam mattress the Navy had managed to discover for ships' bedding. But every fold creased her back, every feather pricked her skin from the ticking in the pillow she always wrapped up over her ears to damp out the noise. It wasn't so much the noise of the ventilation; she had always found the murmurs of a ship rocking in a quiet sea soothing except in this, the XO's stateroom aboard USS *Michael E. Austin*. She would always remember a barely audible tick, click or sometimes even a smack, an erratic nuisance at the end of every gentle roll. Most times it didn't bother her, but that night it had been too much. She looked for its source again, but could not find it. Nor would she ever find it and she would remember that tick, from time to time. It would recur in her thoughts much more often than the image of the ship's captain, wet, elated, somehow thinking that jumping over the side would be to the ship's benefit.

The rumor of the captain's stunt had already filtered into the atmosphere of the Navy's self-knowledge. Junior officers were already calling him Captain Oscar. The chief's mess, always less cordial, had preferred to mark him as the Man Overboard Dummy. Soon, the commodore would be told by someone. Usually, he would hear from an admiral who would hear it from the force master chief who would be told by the ship's senior enlisted man, the command master chief or CMC. The CMC had said as much when he and the XO talked before hitting the rack; he had told the XO she needed to get the captain to report his own actions to the commodore.

But how would the captain see that? Would it be disloyal? Worse, how would the Navy see it? An XO who turns her captain in for a foolish, idiotic (What on earth was he thinking?) trick like jumping over the side would be seen as disloyal. Especially a woman officer. She would be a tattletale, the little girl in the playground who has to tell teacher about boys being boys. And there was no reason to promote tattletales to their own command. But if she didn't tell someone, she would be seen as shirking her duty. Just another girl who doesn't have the guts to do the right thing.

The XO was accustomed to finding the captain at dawn in his chair on the bridge—shined up, full of energy, ready for the day's events. But that morning the XO found her captain in his sea cabin aft of the pilothouse where the sounds of the watch could be heard, but the sunrise left unnoticed. The captain crabbed his chair away from his desk, pointed a lean little finger for her to sit in the sea cabin's couch. Above him and scattered over the bulkheads, the captain had installed pictures of all the ships he had served aboard. There were fourteen: frigates, an old oiler, an aircraft carrier, cruisers, destroyers. So many ships. He'd served on a ship for every year the XO had spent in the Navy. What right did the XO have to think she should judge this guy? But she had.

The captain told her, "XO, I'll be heading over to see the commodore as soon as we tie up this afternoon. I'd like you to stay on board until I get back this evening. You don't have anything to do this evening, do you?"

"No, sir."

"The commodore wants to talk to me about the man overboard drill." Her captain leaned back, twisted his wedding ring.

"I'm sorry, sir."

"So you reported it?"

"No, captain. But I'm sorry it turned out..." She didn't know how to finish that sentence.

The captain did not smile. He did not move. He did not seem to be anything at all except present. "Maybe it was a bit too colorful. I wouldn't blame you if you reported it."

"I didn't."

"I believe you. What would you have done if I hadn't told you the commodore wanted to see me?"

"I think. I think..." The XO wiped her chin with her hand as if she might be able to stop saying anything. "I think I would have asked you to talk to him about it. Because, sir, you see. Someone would tell him about it. Certainly. Someone."

"And it wouldn't look good if you were, what would you call it, covering up?" He had a bulldog sort of face, like his pit bull, only sadder, drier, older.

"It doesn't have anything to do with me, sir."

The captain sat up straight and turned to his desk, his back to the ship's second in command. "Fine XO. That will be all. I won't be needing you on the bridge during sea and anchor detail. Why don't you head aft to square away those line-handlers on the fantail? In fact. You do that XO. You go to the fantail and make sure that goddam chief boatswain gets his lines over smartly and send the first lieutenant on up to the foc'sle where I can keep my eye on him. Because I don't need to keep my fucking eyes on you, do I? Dismissed. Go do some work, or whatever it is you girls do."

The first commanding officer of USS *Michael E. Austin* never returned from his call on the commodore, and USS *Michael E. Austin* realized they would no longer be known as the newest, finest, best ship in the fleet. They would be known as the ship whose commanding officer had been dumb enough to jump over the side to test their man overboard procedures. They would never again be Awesome Austin, or even just All Right Austin. They would be, instead, Oscar.

The future strike group commander took down the pictures of ships bolted to the bulkhead of the captain's sea cabin and thought through the other things she might do with her life, law school, real estate, maybe she could go into banking. Maybe have babies. That would be nice. It would be something. But all she'd ever done after college was serve in the Navy, straight out of Vanderbilt to officer candidate school, one of the first women commissioned to become a surface warfare officer, only to wind up packing her captain's personal effects because the Navy doesn't always let former commanding officers back on board when they do something as stupid as jump over the rail on their own ship.

She never imagined, never expected to rise any higher in rank and that she would always be the XO of the Oscar. All she saw was the end of her career as she sorted through holed underwear, yellowed t-shirts, the still well-pressed uniforms, found the pornography in the bottom drawer of her captain's desk, grimy pages stapled together to display a set of over-exposed pictures, women and men straining in any number of improbable positions. These she threw into the trash, then thought the better of that and piled them up to throw out into the dumpster on the pier herself. The crew had seen enough of their captain's true character. And now, anything about the captain and anything that happened to USS *Michael E. Austin* would be known.

Until the Navy forgets.

The strike group commander does not tell anyone about packing up her captain's personal effects. She tells the FWO and the eavesdropping watch this: "I'm the last Plank Owner of USS *Michael E. Austin* on active duty. That's it. Probably the only person on active duty who remembers Captain Oscar."

She looks up and catches the CNN satellite picture of USS *Michael E. Austin* near an orange lifeboat. The lifeboat dead in the water, the ship near, waiting, and she decides to say, "So here I am, watching the USS *Michael E. Austin*, like everyone else in the blogging, emailing, satellite coverage universe."

"She'll make good, Admiral."

"Oh, I know she will. Butch. I'm not worried."

This is not true. Her doubts about that ship, her memory of the tick in her stateroom as she rolled, these are things she cannot express. And this she will forever keep to herself, both her worry and her sure knowledge that if she had been a better XO, her captain, the man who had been her friend and teacher, would have become a much better strike group commander than she, a naval officer who would be forgotten as quickly as the Navy had forgotten the reason USS *Michael E. Austin* had always been the Oscar, Flag Oscar, Austin Overboard, Awful Austin, now alone on her mission, her future, and all the dog watches to come.

EFENDIM

MUSTAFA WAS THE ONE they chose to speak. The interpreter said he was uneducated, his Arabic very poor, and he had only Coca Cola English. But someone had bequeathed him a sense of dignity, or at least propriety, and it came through in that special tongue of their clan and place, a useless language, one spoken only along their barren coast. Of course, all of them had been chewing khat for God knows how many days. Even after we'd waited through the night, the drug's brilliant grip had not loosened. It helped that the wind veered before midnight, leaving its desiccation and dust behind to come from the open ocean, still vigorous, but cleaned and breezy. We drank it in like fresh water, those in the lifeboat began to seem alive, and by daybreak we thought they may have finished their slide back to the world of real heat and real consequences. We called to them with the loud hailer. They answered, as we suggested, on the boat's radio.

They had been in the water nearly thirty-six hours, three boys, one of them hurt, with their hostage, an older man who spoke no language other than his own. The youngest boy had been hurt badly, his hand crushed in a door as the tanker's crew fled into the engine room. We thought of calling him Rasul, but Mustafa told us to use Fouad. The interpreter thought this revealing, the choice of 'Heart' over 'Messenger.' We think it had no probable significance; it was simply a name he admired. There would never be any indication he knew what it meant or cared.

All this about their names is part of the way it always goes. They think it wise to make up an alias. They imagine it gives protection to their families or even themselves. But without names, they are called Skinny One, Two and Three. Negotiation always demands more and it is never wise to make one's adversary into an object. We had the interpreter choose, and they agreed those names would be acceptable. The oldest one took 'Amir' because he seemed older, even though he did not have the best manner to lead them. Clearly, the smoother one who took radio had the best sense of events and he accepted that name, Mustafa, "the one who was chosen." Of course, when we reach agreement about anything, even their names, the first step in negotiation is past. That is the art of negotiation with those like Amir, Mustafa and Fouad.

As happens, once they had been named, there were needs. There is food on such lifeboats and water. But they wanted rice, more water. Fouad's pain came to the surface after the khat thinned away with sun, time and boredom. We coaxed Fouad to leave for a bit, come to aid on board the ship, stay only as long as it would take to be tended. We will give him back when they wish. They have the hostage yet. We will do as they wish. The captain sent the ship's rubber-hulled boat panting slowly across to them.

It was bad work for the ship's boat at first. The wind shift chopped the sea surface enough to keep the boats too unsteady to bring together without damage. We had the boat's crew cleat a painter to the lifeboat's bow, pay it back to the destroyer's stern where it was made fast. A gentle pull from the destroyer's lightest forward bell steadied it. The gig married up, took away this boy, left water and something for their hunger, returned to the ship and all was at rest. The lifeboat draws along behind us and we wait.

The negotiator sees this as a one of those opportune moments to assess our progress. The first thing he assays is that this interpreter is exceptional. He doesn't ape language; he nurtures it into their tongue, gives it an aroma of veracity. As a result, when the negotiator searches his mental library of all the possible actions and options he may take, his thoughts are guided by the belief that this interpreter and his skill may be trusted. Time has given those in the lifeboat enough structure. They have shown an inclination toward cooperation after their transit from day to night then day again. Now that the khat had faded, it seems reasonable to him that everyone will be ready to start their journey to the end. Maybe even agree to go home. The negotiator decides to coax them out with an honored and old benediction. It is a question. He tells the interpreter, "I think that's enough. Say to them: *How do they think this is going to end?*"

The interpreter has to think about this. This is far from his first negotiation. He had felt as though something like this would occur, this phrase, this trick he'd seen before. He considers whether or not he can explain to the negotiator how those words would be heard by these killers, if that's what they are, *killers*, these boys. They have the guns, the threats and the force of killers. The ravings. Even sober and worn from the drug, even with the young boy taken off the boat and aboard our ship, they are defiant. The interpreter is not sure this is the time for that question.

The negotiator is very skilled with many years in this trade. He speaks plausible Arabic, but this language is unlike any language he knows. He does not understand what the interpreter says or hears, and doesn't care. Even if he understood these exchanges, he wouldn't think about the inflections. The sketchiest translation is difficult to do properly. Someone must consider what is to be said; another must determine how to say it. It only works when these two tasks are carried forward properly and in trust. And there is trust, even kinship in it; the two of them squat comfortably on their heels next to each other.

The negotiator waits in silence to let the interpreter think it through. He is comfortable with waiting.

The warship's captain doesn't feel comfortable. He had tried to crouch with them, but he ached from hip to heels. He has to stand, stretch out, move to stay awake, alert. His destroyer is made to clip through the sea and does not keep well with its narrow beam and shallow draft, near dead in the water. He must let the screws sweep beneath the stern with their lightest pulse to touch the lifeboat's bow forward, move it ever so slowly out. The trick is to keep it so smooth they will never realize how far they are from shore. The captain tries to think about the improvement of his position, well out past that grounding water where they'd caught a stroke of terrific good luck to intercept the lifeboat with its engine quit. Luck or not, he and his ship were not made for this uncertain roll in this sea, an apprehensive itch he can't relieve.

The interpreter does not show his discomfort, but he doesn't think he can find a way to tell the negotiator how ill-advised he finds the question, 'How do they think this will end?' What answer could they give?

They are two boys.

Crouched under that canopy, they can't even see the sky, much less the future. What could they conceivably envision, taking their furtive looks from the doorway before they lean out to piss with only the loom of this warship before them— the tanker they'd expected to take, gone—the ocean drawn empty away all around? Inside the lifeboat it is all white, brilliant, the sun ever higher. They'd opened everything they could to let out the heat: the portholes, the doors, the hatches. They would be tired, worried.

The old man they'd taken certainly must suffer. They had demanded handcuffs from the ship to restrain him, obviously because he'd jumped out of the boat on the first day. Perhaps they had been fooled when they took him. Because he was old, they probably assumed he was the tanker's master. And they had probably assumed he would be submissive. In fact, he was the chief engineer, not even that old by our standards and certainly not submissive. As soon as they slept, all of them exhausted at once, he had tried to swim away. Amir woke in time to use his gun. Fortunately, he'd not been hit, only the water. It took all of them to drag him up the steep sides of the lifeboat and back inside. It must have seemed a moment of terrible jeopardy for them, and they had probably expected it, but they had not been shot.

The hours had passed, the sea had calmed. The seabirds drifted by us to see if there was anything to eat.

The captain and his destroyer had been the perfect instruments for the start of all this, a thundering, all-engines-flank night passage to answer the tanker's alarm, all speed and purpose. His execution of that passage had been perfect. We had been able to get the talent on board without a flinch. This is complex and it takes skill; the interpreter, the negotiator, the fire team, all had either parachuted in next to his ship or flown aboard, lowered down from one of the big, distance-eating helicopters. It takes poise to run hard in a mounting sea, pick the team out of the ocean where they drop with their parachute shrouds and equipment. And the luck of having the engine quit, that was the kind of fortune that makes a naval officer's career spin into the stratosphere of notoriety.

The captain wishes now he could make other calculations of time, speed, distance. He stands over these two strangers, a negotiator and a translator, never mind their names— he doesn't know their names, both of them oblivious to his destroyer's unnatural gait, both hunched over as if they were haggling a carpet in a souk. Like bugs, he thinks. Insects in their body armor and battle rattle.

The captain does not usually think of people this way. He is tired. He forgives himself for his short temper. He congratulates himself; he hasn't said anything or seemed unprofessional.

It doesn't help. He looks away from the negotiator and interpreter and their maddening patience, and lets his eye scan up from the deck to the superstructure with its flight deck and flurry of masts, the radar antennae circling. Signal flags and the brilliant ensign snap. All in order. This is a reassuring habit of inspection, to see his ship as it is, call to mind the way it should be, correct any nonconformity. As the negotiator had directed, two black balls hang mid-hoist on a halyard, the international signal for a ship not-under-command. It is a deception; his destroyer still possesses the ability to steer a course, and its engines are still alive. But with those two spheres displayed, no ship will try to assert a right of way or even come near them unless requested. The appearance of debility, even as a ruse, irks him. Deception itself makes him uncomfortable. He concentrates on his inspection again, ignores the false signal. All else seems shipshape, his crew hidden, but on watch, the top-decks silent but prepared.

Of course, from the beginning, we asked Mustafa what they wanted. This is vastly different than asking them how they think things will to turn out. What they wanted allowed them to envision a paradise of return; he said three million and five hundred thousand dollars. A million for each of them. That seemed fair. Maybe they would give the spare half million to the youngest one because he was so hurt. Maybe it was all for their masters. No matter. They had spoken their terms. They had grown more comfortable and this comfort, perhaps only the lack of khat—something had let them decide to give up Fouad to come aboard for treatment of his hand. This concession, their ease, all this had made us more optimistic about the outcome.

The boy Fouad was asked to consider a discussion with his brothers-at-arms, a moment of honesty to convince them that money was of no consequence whatever; there would never be any money, no millions, not even thousands, and they should quit that lifeboat, come to join him in safety and repose. He wouldn't do it.

He remained in sickbay, on his back, strapped to the gurney.

You propose every avenue, explore every path. That is the way to negotiate these things, put the discussion on solid ground. Fouad told us that when he rested enough, when the pain wore away, he would return to the lifeboat. He seemed in no hurry. Neither were we, and the other two did not demand him back. It was easiest to wait.

The interpreter considers the negotiator's question further. How can he inform those boy-pirates that the world now leaned in over their shoulders in shock and anger, that the silence of this ocean is an illusion? The interpreter does not think they understand the indignation, its howling volume, the international cries for justice and demands for action, the hands wringing for the chief engineer's family and the threats, oaths, the *discourse*, blogged to the universe and thrashed to the air by CNN, and France 24, and RAI, and BBC and Al Jazeera...all those minute-by-breathless-minute reports. The President Already Calls the Shots. The Prime Minister Is Alarmed. Legislative Bodies Pass Emergency Resolutions. How to tell Mustafa over this puny hand-held radio there is no possible outcome other than give up—come aboard the warship as if invited? They will be guests. They will begin their path anew. How to tell them any other wish is of no consequence whatever?

But he thinks, perhaps they *do* understand. These boys certainly know how to milk a cow, all in the timing. They can see themselves to be celebrities in the minds and eyes of the world. Not perhaps. They probably understand.

The interpreter does not believe they are ready to answer the question demanded by the negotiator. Not yet. He knows it like he knows the touch of his own skin; they are not ready, sealed sightless with their fear and sweat in their brittle shell.

The negotiator notes they have become careless about the portholes and doors. He feels the interpreter's discomfort, but it does not worry him. He lets these things go their own course. Time allows it, and it stretches before him with such luxury. As long as the lifeboat remains tethered to them, as long as they are alone on this ocean, we know nothing can alter the outcome. They have had moments already when the fire team could have applied their kinetic option. But we are content to wait. When the lifeboat's engine quit, we gained the time we needed. Luck. Never discount luck, we all know that.

The warship's captain lets himself go to the ship's railing. This is what he likes to see, a clear horizon like so many he has seen standing out to the deep ocean troughs they were meant to patrol. He feels the urge to slip this tether, put on a bell, move. It has become a brilliant day, late morning, the decks hot under his feet, but the breeze still cool. It looks like the weather will hold. Stack-gas from the ship's propulsion, the same gas from the same turbines aircraft use with the same oily cut, flits past to catch the captain's breath. Ordinarily he would call up the pilothouse, have the ship brought about for a breeze to sweep away the gas. But he can't. The negotiator is the one who chooses the heading.

He is only the captain, an instrument, his discomfort is unreasonable. He rolls forward on his feet, feels the deck, concentrates on the slight vibration beneath him. He can take comfort from this vibration. Unnoticeable to the others, it reminds him of the ship's engines beneath him. These others do not know how the propeller spins unseen at one revolution a second. Even when the ship seems at rest, the blades spin. As long as their pitch is kept to zero, they will not bite the water to take the ship forward or back. But they are ready; they await only his word to churn into movement. He feels better with this slight mumble beneath his feet. He relaxes himself. He wishes he could sit. But it would be unseemly. Without control (especially without control) he must still appear in command, even if in service of the negotiator, service he must perform, service he ought to welcome.

The interpreter smells the gas also but he does not note it because he is trying to imagine some way to show the senselessness of these artful questions to the negotiator or even to the boys on the lifeboat. These *are* boys. They have no concept of an ending. Why ask them? They have a concept of money, perhaps their mothers, and certainly the wives money would bring them. They may have a concept of cars and the Nike track suits they wear. He does not know what to say. Worse, he knows he will be re-interpreted later, all of those errors of commission or omission recorded for us to flesh out and fill in, any lie will turn on him, any prevarication will be revealed. But he must try, even if he only appears to act as directed. It can't be this question the negotiator wants of him, the one that will only baffle and confuse and panic.

The interpreter says, "In the name of Allah, the Beneficent, the Merciful." Unaware of any god these boys might have ever believed, he says, "I beseech you to give up your weapons and let them take you onto this ship. They will kill you otherwise. All praise is due to Allah, the Lord of the Worlds. The Beneficent, the Merciful." He says this invocation even though it seems false in any language except Arabic.

The radio is silent. We listen, but it is silent.

"You did not tell him what I wanted." The negotiator presses his binoculars to the boat. They are very careless about the portholes. "Ask him the question. 'How does he expect this to end?'" He is used to this from interpreters. Even the best of them depart from the text. But they cannot help but twist the tone of it; they always reveal their discomfort, their falsehood. It was a simple question, simply put and this is the time for it, he is certain. He does not think his sense of timing comes from his years raising his two boys through their entitled adolescence. He thinks this question comes from *all* his experience, from his decades imagining the function of disparate minds, from his studies into terror's assessment, his many observations of the panic of acts, the impulse gone wrong, the intent misunderstood, the flinches of God—always those—and sometimes the illusions of faith. And, never forget, the visceral pump of the hostage's impulse. At least he has a good hostage—imagine the stones on that old man, a leap out of the boat to swim for it! The negotiator admires him for that and does not want to let him die for it. But the jeopardy is extreme; they will kill him, even on a whim, a twitch.

At least he can count on this hostage to hate and fear his captors. He will never identify with them. Different age, race, no shared language. And the tension is good if it doesn't go too far. Anything to make that lifeboat worse for them is an advantage, even an unreliable hostage. They never expect heat and lassitude and boredom, teenagers. He is certain the time is right to ask them the question he has so often brought to these moments of stasis, to splinter them open to their finish. How do you think this is going to end? They are at the point where any finish will do. All teenagers are the same.

He says to the interpreter, "Well?"

"I did tell them." The interpreter's experience does not allow him the believer's comfort in such ideas as all teenagers are the same. Perhaps some think all are equal in the eyes of God, perhaps it is true, but the interpreter is the medium between differences. He considers this question, this notion, this sly trick—it is naïve, foolish and therefore dangerous. He knows he will not be understood if he tries to explain to the negotiator. He says, "I told them in a manner they would understand."

The negotiator looks back into his binoculars. They feel safer. As the day heats, they will stand more often. It is habit, now. "What did you tell them?"

"I told them for the grace of God, they must surrender or they will be killed."

The warship captain hears this. It surprises him to realize he had expected them killed by now. Maybe he'd already thought of them as dead. Was that the source of his anxiousness, thinking it finished and time to leave? It is a dangerous distraction, thinking of these things. He wishes he could think of some detail he'd forgotten, some preparation he'd overlooked. What had he expected? No chance of a killing? What about the hostage? It all seems impossible to him he could be stopped like this, to squat in this water to wait. Only to wait. What can he do? There is nothing. Nothing he can do with this great engine spinning beneath him; potent, but useless, useless.

This is what he learns at that instant: desperate to occupy himself, surprised that he somehow has let this be a surprise, his eagerness, then he is ashamed to be so unprofessional, so weak—and he learns in that instant to imagine the rosary. He would practice this again many times as he aged and found himself in more and more positions where he was no longer the officer who conducts the operation, no longer the one who orders the rudder or the sweep of a ship's screw, merely the one who watches, guides, judges as his subordinates exercise their functions and complete their missions. He would carry a rosary in his pocket ever after, track it with his fingers, just as the interpreter touches beads he keeps in his pocket to praise Allah, and the negotiator rubs a pink cancer bracelet to let the memory of his wife calm him. Just as the chief engineer in the white interior of the orange lifeboat twists his wedding ring to think of his children, their pictures long away on the ship that had left him, and just as Amir tickles the safety of his derelict gun on and off, watching.

This makes the chief engineer think, Fuck them. They *will* kill him—or some fucking commando would kill him by mistake, but fuck them. Fuck them all. Especially fuck them with their fucked-up Kalashnikov with the stock half the fuck apart.

He'd been astounded the gun had actually worked. The water ripped open so near to him. But the rusty pistol surely didn't work. If it had, he knew Mustafa would have killed him two days before. On his knees with the barrel against his head, the brittle skin over his kneecaps had ground into the deck as he watched his ship's Master tremble. And *he'd* trembled, a grown man, literally shook, his fingers trembled, head. Mustafa garbled something, a crazed child not able to utter a syllable of use as the Master of the tanker begged, his hands up, "Don't shoot him. Yes, yes, we'll do what you need, but what is it?" The chief engineer had crushed every wish he could have ever wished into one blind word of panic, to beg for his own life, but he had been too frightened to speak. He thought he could feel Mustafa trying to make the trigger work, to kill him. The boy raged like a lethal marionette. The gun barrel drilled against his head. His whole lower body loosened, hopeless. He sensed the strike from the steel barrel against his head, the bullet's puncture into his skull. He was an engineer, he trusted cold fact and physics and it came over him like the last spit from a spigot gone dry, it made no difference – he was dead.

He knew it.

It was a moment of surprise, then regret, then there was no word for it. Something opened in him, flowed away, cleared him and washed him clean. A breath, a heartbeat, a closure of his eyes to open them again, a blink, and he was calm.

Calm.

He *was* to die; he knew it. There was the fact that he could do nothing more about it. He had prepared; he was well-insured and his children were grown and happily distant, his wife accustomed to solitude while he cruised in his engine rooms, and now he was almost sixty, still not sick but getting there, never any real success. Chief engineer of a half dozen ships doing a job, paid for one day after the next, one ship after another, and he was going to have to give it up, too old with nothing to leave behind, the only thing he could do, he could try to be like that security guard they'd beheaded on YouTube, the one who said, "Now I'll show you little pricks how to die."

It would go easier for him, no sawing at the neck only the bullet would happen so fast; that was the physics of it, a flash, a blinding light too quick for pain, or fear or anything and— that would be it, except for the unknown, the after; that's what he feared? Why?

He felt so strangely calm.

From his knees, he looked up at the ship's Master. They were friends. He hoped his friend could see the calm moment in his eyes. Perhaps that's why the Master had been able to scramble away while the boy struggled to make the gun work. Perhaps their eyes touched enough to let the Master leave him, disappear out the escape hatch, the boy unable to shoot him, the others too late with the Kalashnikov, and the chief engineer felt glad he was the only one left.

They'd dragged him to the lifeboat, forced it into the water, made him start the engine and it quit. They drifted, slept as the drug oozed its way out of them. He'd seen their exhaustion as a chance and sprang from that calm moment over the side. He'd kicked and pumped, the blood fired through him, his clothes gripped him, his shoes like stone. He wished he could take time to untie them, let his feet kick them free. He would be able to stretch out, scissor his legs into the crawl he remembered he had once been able to do. He wished he could shed all of it, naked, he would angle away through this water away like some brilliant perch, and he knew these wishes were useless. His feet clubbed the water until Amir shot the gun. All the nerve spilled out of him. He floundered back to the boat, flailed the last yard, his arms useless, clumsy, and even grasped by the two boys, he almost failed to climb his way back up the boat's steep freeboard. Exhausted, all of them, they had lain between each other on the bottom of the boat, waiting for the assault that did not come.

Handcuffed, subdued, his skin chaffed and hair stiffened from the dried salt, the heat stinging his eyes, he hears the interpreter's question. He does not understand a word, neither the question nor Mustafa's answer. But he knows the meaning when Mustafa looks across at Amir who shakes his head *no* as he jacks the safety off and on and Mustafa answers, spitting the words out, bitter, frightened. The chief engineer does *not* know them, those on the ship. What is he to them? What is he to Mustapha, angry and impatient? They will finally kill him. Since the pistol failed to work, every scent and sense has been a gift, he knows it, and he finds himself even calmer as the true moment nears. He doesn't even think profanity, all the bravado leaves him, trying to swim for it or famous last words, all of it gone, all the wishes depart and his mind forms no words at all as he looks away to feel the water column beneath them, the vast, insentient depth of the ocean, and he is cupped in its unseen palm. It is more than a mere thought. It is the sensation he'd had so many times over the years in his engine rooms as he conducted the machinery to feel the screws drive. He imagines himself, as he has so often, above an unknowable, quiet, welcoming depth, loosed from it. He is grateful for it.

The interpreter turns to look at the negotiator and the captain so they can see his eyes as he tells them, "He says, as long as they have a single bullet left and the ability to lift their last finger, the hostage will be killed—unless we pay."

Sometimes the negotiator has wished he could pay a ransom. He has often lied. He has told others he would pay, a ruse-of-war to bring them out in the open or let hostages free. He has sometimes said no ransom would ever be paid. But there have been times when it would have been useful to actually give them a ransom, give them a moment's illusion before the true ending snaps shut. Or even let them go. He has sometimes wished he was empowered like other negotiators from other States where they retain an option to negotiate a lower price. But he considers this only an emotional reaction, a sign of the burnout negotiators are told to expect. He considers the alternatives and the reality as he believes any professional ought. He believes in his core that criminals such as these pirates must never be given any opportunity of having their hopes realized. And this is true, as we all know, so no one would ever fault him for the words, "Now. Now will you ask it? Ask him to tell us how he thinks this will turn out."

The interpreter closes his eyes to the sun ever higher and hotter, the froth and sparkle behind the warship's stern, the painter's spank on the cool water as it tugs and slackens the serene bow of the lifeboat. He does not want to do as the negotiator tells him. He breathes in the air warmed over the ship's decks. To be truthful, he doesn't know why he resists. It is God's will, he knows, but he wonders if God has some role for him to play at this moment and he wonders what it may be. He lets it go.

He opens his eyes to speak into the radio when he sees a path. He says, "It is the wrong time to ask this of them." He has not been told the negotiator's name or rank so he uses an address from his deepest sense of respect, a word those of the negotiator's faith might think a comic-book term; but a student of Arabic like the negotiator, even if not a believer, might understand its deep connotation of respect. "*Efendim*, give him something for hope."

While the negotiator had faith in nothing but skill, he had not realized the interpreter was Turkish until he heard that usage. *Efendim*, 'My Master,' he had said. As always, this had been a pickup team. He didn't know any of these people except the fire team he always brings. And it makes no difference to him, ever. It is always enough to know what they are, *interpreter, Captain, Hostage, Pirate, Criminal*... he knows what they are, and what they are supposed to do and can judge them as useful or not. The warship's captain, no hindrance— solid enough, calm and direct as opposed to those other captains, the ones preoccupied with book deals, promotion and CNN. Or the hostage, one of the fighters, a good hostage, that's all he wanted—anything but that Stockholm syndrome nonsense; the vaguely obscene, but understandable, kinship between the taken and the takers. Now that he recognized the interpreter as Turkish and now that he believes the interpreter's deference, his concern, his respect for men as well as God, the negotiator decides he might as well use him. He looks back at the boat through his binoculars and says, "What do you have in mind?"

Both boys had stood, their heads visible at the same time in separate portholes.

The tiny speaker curls into his ear, our question, now? But he remains silent.

The interpreter says, "Let me talk to the one who wants to be called Fouad. He has had time to think, to see us. He will assure them. He will tell them to come aboard. He will convince them of our promises, our glamour."

The negotiator watches the boat. "He won't do it. We tried. You tried. He says he won't."

"Bring him to me. Let me talk to him again. Let them see him on the ship. Perhaps he is related to one or the other. He could be too ashamed to speak. If they see him, perhaps they will give up."

The negotiator stands, stretches his arms. Why not? He'd considered another try at it, but he'd given up hope. He had to admit this. It didn't help that in his ear ever more frequently the fire team let him know they had the targets grouped. If he said the right word, he would be able to count silently down and it would be all over except the instant when they would be taken together at the mental digit zero. It had begun to seem mechanical to him. The right moment, the right instances, the right rule of engagement, the right word and the right people, *fini*. Everybody go home. 'Only say the word and I shall be healed' is an old-time fire team joke.

He looks at the warship captain, raises his eyebrows, but before he can speak, the captain says, "I'm on it—I'll get him," and relieved to be able to do something, anything, he gives a sailor the command.

The negotiator watches Fouad come slowly to him between the two sailors on guard. He is freed of manacles. His guards are unarmed. It is all part of the subterfuge, this appearance of freedom. Yet it is not; what can he do in any case?

He squints in the light. The interpreter says something. Fouad nods and the interpreter hands the radio to him. The boy has no difficulty with its use. He is obviously accustomed to such equipment and at his trial we would cite this notation to indicate he had probably pirated other ships to offset the advantage he had before the jury with his age. He would continue to insist he was sixteen, but we thought him older. It's hard to tell and who knows the truth about them, anything at all, age included?

The interpreter confirms Fouad's message and the tapes later confirmed the interpreter. They were not brothers, but they were closely associated, and Fouad obviously wished them mightily to give up, come aboard the warship. They had been left by others, only three of them, abandoned on the tanker without real hope. It seems probable Foaud felt ashamed his injury had forced them to quit their assault on the oiler. But he said even with the injury, they might have stayed aboard if Mustafa hadn't decided the merchant ship's crew had been too aggressive, too *impolitic*, no…too rude to control with only the three of them, one hurt.

Fouad stands at the destroyer's transom, waves across to the others; we watch them wave back, now in complete trust of the circumstances and their control, they have come this far so the negotiator is prodded again. But he does not speak and silence in itself is an order. The interpreter says, "They will consider it. They will think about your proposal to bring them aboard."

The interpreter then decides to say something he knows to be true, but does not wish to say. He only speaks, in the end, because he knows the negotiator thinks the same thing. "They will pay for time, now."

The negotiator says, "I think so, too. They think they'll get reinforcements."

"That's not good," says the warship captain. "Does that happen? Do they get reinforcements?"

Neither the negotiator nor the interpreter say anything. The captain is about to press the question; he is *not* usually ignored. But he does not speak. It makes no difference whether or not he knows their habits. Habits are no longer of consequence.

Fouad turns his back on the others, shrugs. This needs no interpretation, no other words, this shrug. The interpreter says, "He wants to go back to the hospital."

"He doesn't want to talk to his friends anymore?" says the captain.

"No. They have said farewell."

This is the moment we realize they don't expect to live and now, the rules change.

The interpreter squats again to consider his words, what he has done and what he has failed to do. The negotiator lowers himself next to him to consider the options left with the lifeboat. The captain leans over to be close. None of them see Fouad walk away, eyes on his own feet, guards on watch over him. In the negotiator's ear there is a conversation about reinforcements enroute. There is a discussion of imminent danger, threat and risk. The negotiator listens, but he does not have to say anything and the discussion stops until the fire team pricks his ear with the opportunity. Amir and Mustapha look very comfortable near the windows.

They *are* more comfortable. The chief engineer can see it. He had been handcuffed to a rung of a ladder step on the lifeboat's bulkhead. They were careful to place him where he could lean back, lie down on the seat. He does not understand why the handcuffs were given to them. He thinks they should have been refused and does not know how important it is to have him fixed in place. But even if he had known, the shackles would have bothered him. The gun was one thing, but dragged down by a boat or ship—that was a nightmare from a lifetime's imagination nurtured deep in his ships' engine rooms. Death he could manage, but irony, no matter how elegant, he could do without.

And he can't breathe, caught like this in the fierce heat of the lifeboat's bow where they had put him far enough away so he could no longer spit on them, for glory, balls or even entertainment. They had been very cagey. When they'd gotten water and food, they'd had the chief engineer try it first. He refused, but they forced him to do it. One of them pinched his ear with a pliers from the boat's tool kit until he tasted it, then spewed it on them. They'd used the pliers again to make him swallow. They waited a half hour. He thought he might feign loss of consciousness, but he knew they would use the pliers to test him. Nothing happened. They ate, drank and shared with him.

Now the two are relaxed and it irritates him. He can't even stand. As long as he is to die, why couldn't they give him some air? They can see he is breathing poorly. Why couldn't they move him closer to the window? It had been a mistake to taunt them. He closes his eyes. He smells one of them, a weedy, sour smell, and opens his eyes to see him use the key on the handcuffs. He is brought to a high seat where he can get his head above the windowsill, take in a breath. They fasten him to a stanchion, "Thank you," he says in his language. He tries to remember it in Arabic, "*Shukran*," he says, and nods. Supposedly, they nod back.

What makes them lie? "*Shukran*." How would he know it, that word? Even if he knew it, would he say it? But they all lie, and it makes no difference, none at all. We pull apart these reports, pick them over for some nugget of fact, listen to all the bleating after-action denials, and confessions, and reconstructions. We don't even wonder anymore why some of them give up and others die. What fable do they hear, what story whispers itself to lull them, then beckon them across? The ones in the markets with the chest wrapped in C-4. The car full of fertilizer, gas and crazed adrenalin. These are instants in a chain of instances, real movement. Belief, always belief—but this? We never know about this sort, these boys the chief engineer says were as relaxed as the air wandering through the porthole. And lie or not, the chief engineer will say it enough times that he will come to believe he said it, *Shukran*.

But they do bring him to the open hatch where he tastes the salt and sun-cleansed sea breeze. He breathes out, lets go again and sees Amir and Mustapha watch him with their brown eyes and thin collar bones, every ligament on their necks visible. Amir's heart speeds, his pulse, so quick and close to the skin. They are intent, these two. This is the way of it. The ship's transom seems both near and far and he knows perfect firearms focus with precision on the porthole where his vague silhouette is a shadow. He notes like the observance of the weather, or a time of day, or the color of water—incidental and not important—that this will be his execution.

The chief engineer no longer measures his past and no longer follows any literal memory. His every sense is opened, aware of the sea breeze, the stares of his murderers, of the gentle shove of this boat, its brilliance and heat, those who will kill him, those who will mourn him, but he is no longer of it. He is not surprised. He is not grateful. He is something other than mere sense, swept on without time, beyond depth, past any expectation.

The radio speaks to Mustapha and Amir.

The negotiator had prodded the interpreter, "Now we should ask him."

"Yes." He clears his throat, lifts the radio, and he envisions his own sons. "God is great. In the name of Allah, the Beneficent, the Merciful. You must answer this—how is it you foresee the end of this moment?" He stands. Soon the midday prayer will turn them to the sun's decline. It will be done by then, he knows. "You must answer, what do you believe will become of you?" He cannot find the right words, but he can think of no other means to ask. "What do you believe God's plan divines for you, now?"

The interpreter looks up to the horizon where he knows other warships wait beyond to converge on this quiet piece of the ocean when it is done. The captain raises his face to the sky and the sun's high heat, and the negotiator can feel it as well. The breeze had veered again to sweep the stack gas away over the side and from under the loom of the superstructure where the fire team speaks and counts heads and we watch every minuscule shadow.

Mustafa and Amir are more careless about the portholes.

The fire team is not careless.

The fire team will always call the two left in the boat Skinny One and Two with Skinny Three in the bag. The fire team will not change the names during any operation with the outcome still unknown. And nothing has been decided yet. Other pirates had been in Germany and released. Another had gone to New York and had become a sort of celebrity. Surely they know this. But they do not answer. They do not say anything. They no longer speak, no longer communicate at all

Amir lies on the seat of the lifeboat in the brilliant white under the heat where he looks at Mustafa slouched in the seat across. Amir still has the broken Kalashnikov. But Mustafa has left the useless pistol unattended near the transom. The man they thought was the ship's master remains alive where they left him, handcuffed near the porthole. After a while, the men with the gig marry up to let other men come on board with their arms and caution. They release the chief engineer, mute, stiff and by appearances, unharmed. They help him to the warship and safety where he meets the warship's captain and they greet each other in joy. Their picture together is taken, a snapshot for the internet.

Before they remove Amir and Mustafa, official photographs are made. These photos would remain secret for a time. But after people no longer cared about what had happened, they would emerge where the people who wished it could take pleasure in their squalor.

The chief engineer was to be celebrated for his safe return and his courage, and the logic of the whole event was constructed to go like this: the chief engineer was well-liked by all the men on the tanker who had been able to flee to the engine room. The Master was always sorry he had abandoned him, but they both agreed it had probably saved the chief engineer's life. If there had been two, one would have been shot to make a point. It would have been the chief engineer, older and less consequential, only useful if he was the sole hostage.

Sole hostage or not, they probably *would* have killed him, in the end. Or perhaps, they would not have. The negotiator is used to such ambiguity in outcomes, accustomed to their placement far from him where he will never return to visit. He packs up to leave the scene, as he does, with hopes the next one will be as painless. There will be fewer of these events due to this outcome. The range of probable results will be more dreaded and the promise of paradise less certain. But the team doesn't care about this. They care about their return home, and it isn't easy. A helicopter lily-pads to shore, first to one ship then another for fuel, finally feet dry and gone.

As the interpreter watches Fouad in the aircraft, he prays he has done the right thing in the eyes of God. But he is not sincere about this. He knows he did the best thing he could. He never deceived them, never thought he had told them an untruth. He had no foreknowledge of the sniping and without him, they never would have been able to save this boy.

Fouad is shackled and he leans forward on his straps alone.

He will be tried in our court somewhere by someone and interrogated in some manner. His guards have taken their places about him, too far to be touched, near enough to touch. They are masked and helmeted anonymities who will never be known to those who will soon see Fouad's face posted under screaming magazines, blogs, official reports and broadcast speculation: "The Face of Terror." Fouad will have a real name, soon, and there will be some family constructed, a past, a future, a present. He will never leave us now, and perhaps that was God's will, the interpreter thinks. Perhaps that is the sense of it. Fouad's eyes flit about the long rib cage of the helicopter, its naked hydraulics, its tiny ports, its benches full of the men who had caught him and killed the others. He does not look afraid to the interpreter who continues his prayer for mercy. Maybe if he had not performed as he had, the hostage would have been killed. But he knows, as it was, as it will be. God wills it. He is not sincere and he asks forgiveness for this, and for himself.

The warship's captain leaves Mustafa and Amir on the lifeboat, as ordered, until the flagship comes, equipped for decedent affairs with its body bags and morgue to take them away. That ship cranes the lifeboat up out of the ocean and onto its flight deck where there will be an investigation. Later it will go to a museum, then to storage when the museum is no longer of interest. The press pool arrives and the captain starts his journey into the airwaves and internet, his promotion, and the dream he will have from time to time. It will return in different guises but it will always feature a decoration. He wears it, but does not recognize it. He is allowed it, but knows it must belong to someone else.

The press pool left after taking all they wanted, and there was nothing to do but set the destroyer to its normal passage, relieved and comfortable, finally able to imagine themselves free to let the engines drive where they would go with their accustomed grace.

The chief engineer never loved his captors; we were right about him. He never once thought of them as if they were his own sons or imagined himself in their positions. But he, too, has his dreams and these boys return to him, suddenly still in the white lifeboat with the shocking copper taste in the dead air, both their heads skewed, their eyes closed. He hears Mustafa's last exhalation, a child's signal of boredom as he comes to rest, his shoulders collapsed, frail and broken—and this is the part we know is true—he dreams it over-and-over until it becomes part of the life he'd given up living. He forgets that calm moment when he'd seemed inconsequential—and he heaves his way up from the empty basin below the lifeboat; he kicks and pumps, his blood fires through him, his clothes bind and twist around him, ever tighter they squeeze, his feet turn to stone, he clubs them without purchase into the water, reaches up to claw at the boat's high freeboard. He is alone. Ever weakened, he struggles against it, that pull, that corporeal draw.

This we believe is mostly true.

CASTOFFS

DANICA LEARNED TO SHOOT from her father, a cop, who, seeing his tiny adolescent daughter pine for a horse he could not provide, asked her mother, "Why is it young girls love horses so much?" The woman who had managed to come up with enough money to teach their daughter to ride the rangy, worn horseflesh of their town, all of five feet two inches tall as Danica would prove to be, reached across the sheets to take his hand. "A horse is a big, powerful animal, totally devoted to someone who is small. You step *up* on a horse, high over anyone else—until she finds someone like you for herself, she'll want that horse."

He stared up into the dark, squeezed her hand, "I see," and took fourteen-year-old Danica to the civilian range where he went to practice instead of drinking when he felt like drinking.

She loved shooting from the start. The warm feel of the grip, its enthusiastic kick, the neat holes in the paper. She loved the scent, feral, like a skunk when you don't get too much of him. She loved the smooth mechanism of an automatic pistol, every slot and groove machined to a perfect purpose and the glitter of brass going into the clip, the warm touch of the casings when she policed them off the concrete floor of the range, as her father taught her to do.

After she shot a perfect score at boot-camp, after we trained her and made her into a gunners mate, and after she had gained experience booting a shell the size of a sewer pipe out of a destroyer's main battery, she became the master of the two crew-served, Model 242, 25mm chain-fed auto-canons on board USS *Michael E. Austin*. An auto-canon: pull the trigger and it coughs out an explosive round the size of a tent stake every quarter second. Crew-served: you aim it by eye and hand. The Marine Corps calls that gun the Bushmaster, the Navy calls it the chain gun, and everybody agrees it's a sweet piece of work.

Except for rust.

We like the word corrosion better than rust. It seems more civilized. But Danica had no such illusions. Rust had been her father's word, the *rust* he had taught her to hate and fear—a single fingerprint could etch a gun's bluing if not properly oiled over, the smallest spec of powder residue can ruin the lands and grooves of the rifling and destroy any gun's accuracy. Think of her chain guns exposed to the sea air, bolted to the main decks, a flimsy canvas tied over them. Think of Danica's worry over the daily spurt of salt air or worse, a storm—one of those great storms born at sea from heat and the clean fetch of wind, current, sun and time—it beat their ship, forced the captain to close the weather decks. Her guns lay near naked, the storm spawning a cancer of rust on their tiny organs.

Finally, as all storms do, it veered off and found a shore, the hovels and skeletal remains of Mogadishu. The wind and seas abated enough to allow Danica topside, first out on deck with her maintenance cards, her oils and her greases, her brushes and tools and her striker, Seaman Apprentice Yan, both of them suited up in the body armor and helmets demanded of maintenance on a live gun. Logs would note a grey dawn, the wind astern, a rolling ocean underfoot. She worked while the ship stood slowly through a low, dense haze near the surface of the ocean. Soon, she grew calm, full of satisfaction that her chain guns were intact.

We had thought that after the bad weather, the clans, the former fishermen, the residue of failed governments—all the bad actors—would be hunkered down, piracy at a halt, their flimsy skills made helpless. *No activity* had been the intel guys best assessment. As for Danica, five months off the coast of Somalia, she had long given up expecting to use her chain gun for anything other than target practice on garbage bags, which was all right by her. Her father had been one of those old-time cops who had never drawn his gun. "Doesn't mean you shouldn't know how. Doesn't mean you shouldn't be ready," he used to tell her while cleaning the steel after their target practice.

After Danica and Striker Yan scoured the metal surfaces, after they oiled, rubbed and worked the mechanisms and cycled the loader with hammer-handle sized dud rounds, Danica declared herself satisfied with the gun's clean, glistening surfaces. She had Yan attach the full bin of live ammunition and was about to secure the barrel into its stowed position when, away off the ship's port bow, something stood up from the sea in the fog. She could barely see it, a crappy fishing boat atop a wave, dim in the mist. She looked down to set the locking mechanism to keep the barrel from swinging around as the ship rolled down to leer over the water, then back to face the air and now, the fishing boat was pointing its bow right at them, closing, less than a thousand yards away.

Danica heard the hollow voice of the general announcing system: *Captain to the Pilothouse.* That little wooden boat was awfully close. A rattle of harsh smacks—two more stinging cracks, steel on steel like a ball peen hammer against the hull. Striker Yan hollered, "There! There!" and pointed to a streak of smoke then a frantic splash, maybe an explosion in the water off the ship's quarter. The boat churned up a wake from an engine belching black, veered away, then stubbed a toe on a steeper swell, and the hull rolled up showing the stained white sides, clumsy wood with a brilliant blue strip. A small cabin on the boat's deck looked as knocked together as the icehouses that used to sink into the lakes where Danica had lived. It was abeam the ship now, and Danica could feel the rudder come over hard left, the bridge watch turning toward the boat.

Easy to see, she thought. But pretty soon it would be bow on, and she wouldn't have a shot. She unlocked the gun, peered into the telescopic sights. "Yan, get on the phones to the bridge!" A bunch of people with scuzzy pirate hoodies and tracksuits were messing around with something on deck. One shouldered some sort of weapon. A rocket-propelled grenade maybe?

She heard Striker Yan holler into the rubber mouthpiece of the sound-powered phones, "Bridge this is mount two-fifty-two. Mount two-fifty-TWO. Bridge? Pilothouse?"

Heartbeats of silence. "This is mount two-fifty-two, can you hear me?"

It *was* an RPG. "RPG! RPG, tell the bridge it's an RPG!"

The guy on the boat's fantail had the cone tip of the grenade pointed toward them. Danica thought, how strange, you *do* get watery knees. Couldn't that guy see the gun pointing at him?

It would not be a difficult shot. She told herself to wait for the deep breath at the top of the swell. Then all Danica felt was the shudder of steel, the battle roar. The tracer of every fourth round arced out too high, and she held the barrel steady to let the ship roll the fire down onto the bobbing wooden boat. She felt eerily calm.

Jim Ehrlich was a standard, solid-citizen naval officer who had never imagined finding himself in command of USS *Michael E. Austin* off the coast of Africa. At this moment in his life, he had expected to be stuck at a desk in a shipyard, a crummy engineering job—or maybe, if he was totally out of luck, the Pentagon. He had expected to be getting over being pissed off that his reward for the year and a half of constant strain it took to bring ancient, old Oscar Overboard back to life in a shipyard would be a butt-numbing and useless life in an office cubicle. He had weathered all the disappointments and surprises hidden inside six thousand tons of twenty-year old steel, cable, aluminum, insulation, fuel and water, sewage and pneumatics. And, as we expected, he had done a fine, fine job.

The fact is, we would have moved Commander Ehrlich on to his shipyard spot and turned over his splendid, refurbished ship with his retrained and ready crew to a more deserving officer. We had an admiral's aide-de-camp in mind, a think-tank savant, one of our brighter stars primed to take on a big job someday.

However, at the last moment, the designated former aide-de-camp found himself waylaid. It could have been anything;

a little run-in with a cop after too much to drink. A little mistake on a travel claim. Subordinates unhappy with a dictatorial manner or perhaps he had been caught doing some sort of unauthorized sex—strange how some people think they get more attractive with higher rank.

Jim didn't know for certain. All he knew was, impossibly, he had been bequeathed six extra months in wondrous command of the splendid combat platform he had brought back to life.

His ship had done very well, running off a half dozen piracy attempts. His crew busy in their housekeeping after the storm, loading, cleaning, briefing and readying for action to come, he could not help himself from feeling pretty good. At least nobody had fucked anything up and Jim Ehrlich wasn't the sort who would make his subordinates unhappy with a dictatorial manner or try to screw one of the enlisted kids, no matter how bored he got.

As for now, it was the hour of letdown, *no activity*, and Jim had left the pilothouse to the watch giving himself a little time in the ship's wardroom where he liked to be seen catching his thoughts in his notebook before he lost them. Lately, he'd been trying to write some tips for those who would come after him in command. The sort of thing that might be published in the Naval Institute Proceedings with a pointed and easy-to-remember title headings such as, "Delegate, Don't Frustrate." In the back of his mind, he was thinking about a book full of those essays. But he'd been thinking lately, wasn't some of it luck? Maybe all of it? Wasn't it luck he was in command, luck that a hostage they'd rescued had lived through it. Maybe he could write a chapter that says, "Not All Luck is Bad"?

The general announcing system clicked once then belted out its hollow demand: *Captain to the Pilothouse.* The ship leaned into a hard port turn, and he felt the screws twist into reverse. Collision. Imminent collision; that's the only reason for such a turn. He slammed out of the wardroom, started running for the bridge when he felt the chain gun's first detonation like a stroke, and he was almost relieved. At least they weren't going to bend steel side-to-side with another ship.

The ship's alarms went off for general quarters, *All hands man your battle stations.* He turned to sprint up the ladders to the pilothouse, sailors exploding down the passageway, hurrying past him, trained, readied.

He stopped. Next to him, out the watertight door, he would be at the gun itself. He flipped up the perfectly aligned quick-acting release levers, all the clever works that had kept a week of blasting seas outside let go precisely as designed, and he stepped out to realize, no, this had not been some stupid mishap he would have to report or an inadvertent discharge of a gun he would have to write up. This was a shot-up and wallowing boat, splintered, stricken, and about to settle forever under a wash of foggy sea. A crazy angled deckhouse, the bow festooned with a drove of crew who'd scrambled to the high point; the XO and the bridge watch were bringing Austin around to close it.

"What happened?" Two of his sailors stared at him like puppies caught pissing on the rug. "Petty Officer Deacon, what the hell happened?"

She shook her head slowly in wonder. "Shot the shit out of them, sir. Shot them."

"Did you get permission to fire from the bridge?" Ehrlich's standing orders said only the captain could grant permission to fire on an enemy.

"They shot at us. And they were going to do it again. Shot them up." Spray on her face. Tears? This was some sort of accident chain, some series of blunders leading to catastrophe.

The seaman behind her said, "The pilothouse never said anything, Captain. And they had their hands up."

The seaman was young. Yan. Korean family. College degree from Long Beach State. On the ship about a year. Maybe he didn't like working for Deacon. A small woman with no college degree, nothing but experience. There were two ways to play this. Yan was giving him an out.

"Is that true? Did they shoot at us?"

Deacon lifted her chin up to him. "Yes, Captain."

His fat, black communicator, his brick, squawked at him from the pilothouse, *"Captain, the port chain gun shot at a boat. Request permission to launch the boarding team."*

Aft, the boat already bustled with armed sailors. "Launch it."

He knew that when his boarding team made it to the sinking fishing boat, there would be no guns on board. Any firearms or contraband was already sinking its two miles down to the bottom of the Somali Basin.

Jim turned to Deacon who jutted out her lower jaw as if she was getting ready to fight, and he decided, looking at her clear-eyed face, you have to delegate. Not all luck is bad. It's all in the story.

"Petty Officer Deacon, you better get back on that gun."

She buried her eyes in the sights and Jim told her, "You saw them loading up, and you took them under fire before they could shoot at us again. You did exactly the right thing." Her shoulders slackened.

"The bridge never gave us permission to fire," Yan told him.

He put his hand on the young woman's shoulder, gripped it. "If anyone ever asks you about it, Deacon, you tell them the captain of your ship said you did exactly the right thing. You tell them to talk to me. And you." He pointed to Yan. "You tell the truth. No matter what. Don't make anything up, hear me?"

"Aye-aye, sir," said the blank-faced boy.

The boarding team and boat crew bounded toward the collection of Somalis standing still with hands in the air. What if it was a trick? What if they had someone ready to shoot?

Then the boarding team would kill them all. Delegate, sometimes you have to give them a little faith. That would be a damn good essay. "Give Them A Little Faith."

The announcing system called everyone to flight quarters. Smart. The bridge watch and XO were thinking ahead. The prisoners, especially any injured would need to be evacuated to the flagship; they were already priming the ship's helicopter to launch.

"You okay, now, Petty Officer Deacon?"

Deacon lifted her eyes from the optics when the boarding team made fast to the pirate's boat. She looked better. She gave him a happy grin, a wild looking thing on this tiny young woman with her fair skin and wisps of black hair curling out. He would never forget it. "Never better, Captain. Scattered their shit, sir."

"Yes, you did." Then he told her what you say in those circumstances. He told her, well done. He said, good shooting.

Deacon pressed her face back into the sights, looked away. Looked again.

"Captain." Deacon sounded small, frightened. "There's a girl on that boat."

Rear Admiral Olivia Luce, Commander, Bonhomme Richard Strike Group, looked down from the aerie of her flag bridge to watch the lizard-faced helicopter from Austin place its dainty feet on the massive flight deck. A crew ran out to the machine before the blades stopped turning and hoisted a stokes stretcher out of the door. A young girl, not seriously injured, Austin had said. Suffering exposure, dehydration, the usual effects of neglect. They hustled the stretcher into the ship with one of the ship's crew following, the health and welfare escort. More like a plausible witness, Olivia thought, someone to contradict any accusations of maltreatment.

Maltreatment.

Olivia stretched herself down from the chair. Ever since the Abu Ghraib pictures of young women leading around naked prisoners in dog collars, you want to check on maltreatment yourself, especially when you are in command of thirty-five hundred sailors and Marines on four ships. You only get what you expect when you inspect, Olivia believed.

She found the thin girl sleeping, the only patient in the ship's intensive care unit, so delicate—the crisp folds of sickbay's hospital sheets seemed capable of injuring her. For an uncomfortable moment, Olivia wondered what it would have been like to have had a daughter. She pushed that thought away quickly enough, these afflictions you cast aside out of habit.

Was the girl cast aside out of habit? Strange how people get these labels: hostage, pirate, captain, admiral, castaway.

All those names somehow making you more or less than what you are.

The interpreter told her the girl came from the border between countries where the notion of food is altered by drought and the shifts of political wind. She had been one of many children in a family, and her father had likely sold her. The girl hadn't known this. She only knew that one afternoon a man in a truck came to take her away, and she was put on a boat with four other girls and eight men. She was fed and kept.

The interpreter was a thin man, Arab-dark with a goatee that made Olivia think of goats themselves. He smelled like black tobacco and age. Then, looking down at the young woman, he spoke as if he had not wanted to say the words, "Admiral. She speaks the same language as the prisoners. Madam, she was their cargo. They tried to sink her before the ship's boat could get to them. There were others."

"How many?"

"She wouldn't say or doesn't know."

Traffickers. Not pirates. Olivia was about to ask what had happened to the other girls, then found herself so wearied and so certain she knew. She pulled a chair next to the bed. What children they are. What a terrible world that they must be so cruelly used. Other women, probably lost. Some of the traffickers dead also. How many? She would never know.

As happens when an admiral decides to become stationary, the cluster of officers and medical personnel grew accustomed to her presence and started to filter away until Olivia found herself alone with the patient and a small, young woman, a girl not much older than the castaway dressed in the blue scramble of camouflaged body armor sailors wear on deck. An M-9 pistol hung impossibly large on her service belt. She wore a USS *Michael E. Austin* ball cap. Obviously the health and welfare escort, a petty officer from her rating badge, Deacon from her nametag. She looked like she wanted to say something. This happened often. When the men left the room, the young women would ask Olivia something about the Navy. Or about herself. She would never escape being a woman admiral. Olivia didn't mind. She wanted to be thought of as a woman. God knows how she became an admiral. Gave up children, she supposed. "Something on your mind, Petty Officer?"

"Yes, ma'am—uh—Admiral." The girl had very clear, brown eyes. Almost green. "What will happen to her?"

"I don't know." Olivia said it as if she was asking the question. "I guess if she's a refugee, then maybe someone will give her a visa. As of now, she's a castaway or something. I suppose they'll repatriate her back to wherever she comes from."

Deacon touched the edge of her patient's sheet. The girl moved, watched Deacon's fingers with wide, brown eyes. "Admiral. Ma'am. What's the difference between a refugee and a castaway?"

Castoffs, all of them, Olivia thought. People who are thrown out like garbage, they are all the same, and you have to ask, why them? Why is it that way? This young sailor, Deacon, lives in a world of men who will kill children and never feel the loss of their souls. Olivia was about to answer with something about the sea and boats. She was about to talk about UN designations of refugees, how they are sorted and called. But she could not, this time. This time she said the bare truth, "I don't know, Petty Officer. People say they know the difference, but they don't."

The Hour of Letdown

The day broke as generous as a caress, even a kiss—summer clouds bumbling in a cheerful sky, what more could she want? All the wind, and spume, and mountain seas had disappeared overnight. They sailed over a well-ordered swell with a long fetch and a lullaby rhythm. She decided it was safe to work out on deck for the first time in a week and let them open the doors after lunch to return the ship to cleanliness and order. All the chaos, gone. Their plunging bow, the lashing spume and seas, seasickness, exhaustion, only a memory. Everything coming back to routine, everyone not on watch turned-to wiping up the spilled coffee, cleaning wet, salted decks, sweeping away all the dirt and dust knocked out of the overhead by the beating they'd taken. All would be in order by sunset. There had been no real damage. No one hurt.

So why this? the XO wonders. Why this feeling that something is going wrong? She likes to tell people, *just the facts, give me the facts*, but she believes in instinct. Fifteen years at sea, you get a feeling for things. Probably fatigue. She had taken her first good shower in four days. Three big bruises. Ship bites. She couldn't remember getting them, but there they were, purple and aching on her elbow, hip, and thigh. She'd hooked up the sports bra, clean t-shirt. Cotton briefs, she liked to think of them. The word *panties* always seemed too girly. A stiff-starched set of coveralls. She'd even used a blow dryer. Usually, she leaves her blunt haircut alone to dry. No sense trying to pretty up a workhorse, but ahhh…the warmth of that blow dryer over her scalp, her neck, over her face, her taut shoulders loosened.

When it had become impossible to work at her desk (it seems like a month ago) she had stuffed a fat pile of paperwork in her file cabinet. But why work in her stateroom office on a day like today? After a rollicking lunch with the other officers, she brought the whole mess up to the pilothouse to work in the fresh air. Why not luxuriate? The last week would soon float away like every other mean-spirited act of God.

But something had felt off from the moment she'd awakened to see the storm blown out, and despite the warm morning in light air, despite the fat comfort of her chair, something around her seems strange. Almost like a bad smell.

What is it?

Not the watch. Everyone in the pilothouse seems relaxed, scrubbed and fed if not well rested. They sway together with the ship's gentle motion. The officer of the deck, Lieutenant "Spike" Marlin, is as sharp and utilitarian as his namesake, the steel marlin spike used to lever open splices in wire rope. Spike, the perfect guy to make her feel comfortable, even with spanky new Ensign Bailey working for him as conning officer to give the ship its helm orders. Not that they had to turn anywhere. Steam slowly on station. Wait for a mission. Wait for something to happen.

Cool air from the open door fingers her bare neck. She can see the ship's helicopter fluttering near the horizon like a little insect. She would have waited to launch, but the detachment commander, Duck, had talked the captain into letting her fly to qualify a new guy, one of her nuggets. So be it. At sea, a destroyer operates. That's what they do. Operate. If Duck Swann wants to play with her toy airplane, let her.

The XO leans forward to let the good warm sun fall broad onto her back and tells herself, what's the worry? Below the pilothouse, sailors firehose thick drafts of fresh water to wash the dried salt off the gun mount. Others skip the runoff into the scuppers with short bristle brushes on broomsticks. Boys and girls. They don't even know how tired they are. Easy to slip on something. Happy, they goof around with the water, flick it at each other. One of them walks on an anchor chain, a boy showing, pretending to be a tightrope walker, all of them wiggling and giggling. Unseamanlike.

Not paying attention. Somebody will get hurt.

And she realizes why she is so uncomfortable: it is the hour of letdown—everyone acting too relaxed. She starts to get out of her chair to kick a little ass, tell them to quit this skylarking, but the chief boatswain's mate bursts onto the foc'sle below her, his blue coveralls stretched smooth on his massive hams. The XO cannot hear what he says, but who needs to hear him, watching him jerk his short radius arm in a circle, stab a finger at the deck? The sailors quit fooling around, get down to work.

That's the way it needs to go: everyone, even the chief petty officers, out and about, looking after their people, a few grownups to shake the sailors out of this hour of letdown. They feel the same unease—let the kids get too relaxed when they are tired, next thing, someone slips off that anchor chain.

Next thing, you get a cracked skull on a steel deck and you're inventorying personal effects to send home to mom and dad.

No wonder she's worried.

Mom and Dad. Her captain would be the ship's dad. The crew had called her Mama-san from the first. Not so bad. She'd been called worse. She had been able to get some rest during the storm, but the captain had not. She's certain he's getting some rest in his cabin, but a boatswain's mate the crew called Pixie salutes her and points at him slouched down in his chair like a disheveled bird. "XO, he's fast sleep. Like a baby."

How had he become invisible? How had she missed him? Now she hears him. Not an actual snore, more of a purr. She had been able to feel his exhaustion all week, thick as wet wool. All through the dirty weather, she had watched him nod off despite the ship's jerky rhythm only to be awakened by the OOD for some report or another. A new ship on the horizon. Some issue with the weather itself. A call for every turn. But he brought it on himself; she thought, those are his standing orders to his officers. Call when in doubt and doubt there had been. Visibility near zero. She put her hand on the vinyl armrest of his chair, close enough to feel his warmth, his whole body a collapsed collection of sticks.

"Captain, sir."

"Hmmm? What is it XO?" He lifted his head up as if it was too heavy for his shoulders.

"Sir. You were snoring."

"I was?" She loved that smile. She would always tell people he'd had an amazing knack for making you feel like you were both trusted and watched over.

"I guess that's not so good, the captain snoring on the bridge." He raised his voice to let the watchstanders hear him.

He was not the sort of man to keep secrets. No whispering, he liked to say. Never let anyone think there are any secrets. "We don't want anyone sleeping in the pilothouse, do we XO?"

"No, sir." The whole watch shuffled in delight behind her.

"So, XO, do you think I could go below and catch a nooner?"

"Sir, a nooner is everyone's God-given right." The watch smiled in appreciation of that well-known, unofficial regulation from their XO. The Navy Nooner—a half hour stolen before going back to work after the midday meal when sailors took off their shoes, stretched out in their racks for the quick nap they'd earned through the watch they'd stood the night before.

"Very well, then. I shall go to my sea cabin—*Officer of the Deck!*"

"Sir." Everything about Spike radiated pleasure and relaxation. All you need is a happy captain, and you have a happy ship.

"I shall be in my sea cabin performing official functions. Call me for any change in the status of the aircraft. Make your other reports to the XO."

"Aye, aye, sir."

Boatswain's Mate Pixie sang out: *Captain is off the bridge.*

The quartermaster logged: *Captain departed the pilothouse.*

The XO took her seat on the other side of the pilothouse satisfied that her captain believed the ship could watch over him for a minute or two. And she could watch over the ship.

She tried to read the first piece of postponed administration at her little foldout desk. Internet be damned, the Navy was still going to create papers like this—long, thickly written and too dull for the fine weather. She made it to a paragraph that said something about reordering institutionally issued equipment before the end of the quarter, and her sense of unease drifted away into the morass of bureaucratized language, then faded and it was gone.

Now, this.

And *this* is Spike waking her up out of a dead sleep, "XO. I'm setting flight quarters." And *this* is fog pressing against her face, blinding, suffocating. It lolls filaments across every surface, fills every corner, dampens every sound. A destroyer's pilothouse is high out of the water, and in fog like this, the world disappears. She cannot see the ship's bow. She cannot even see the surface of the ocean. They are blind.

And *this* is a helicopter in the air with limited fuel and three souls on board, too far from any shore. The XO feels the captain come up behind her. She does not realize she had left her chair to grip the post under the compass repeater as if it was the only thing that could hold her up. "Captain. It was fine. Then. It was like this, no warning. Spike has called away flight quarters. I had him come up to a flight course to take the bird back on deck."

She feels him drawn as tight as wire next to her. "Dew point, XO. We weren't watching the dew point separation. It cooled off with the sun getting lower down."

The captain picks up the radio handset microphone. All the watch stations hear him, "Bumble Bee Two One, this is the CO, over." Something about his voice, full of confidence. Full of poise. Nothing to worry about. A little low visibility.

"Roger, sir. Here's our sitrep…" The speaker disembodies her. Lieutenant Swann. The XO pictures her in that impossibly big helmet over those delicate shoulders. Her voice has a little vibration in it. A mechanical sound to her, the aircraft's vibration. Not any panic. Or is it? Duck Swann, the Ugly Duckling. She starts to sound less certain and now, the watch is beginning to look at each other. She finishes and it's not procedure. She says, "…we've only got a half hour bag of fuel more or less, over."

"More, or less? Which, Swann? Over."

"A half hour." Now she sounds worried. "I can see the ship's mast. It's all clear air up here. But you're in the…" They hear her take a breath. "Fog."

It's a rotten air, wet. All sound muffled. Could be worse. The XO glances at the captain whose lips tighten. Their eyes meet, and he says, "Can you see the ship well enough to make an approach? Over."

"Ahh, roger, sir. We could try. But we're out of qualification for low visibility."

"Ok. I know, I know."

Out of qual. She wouldn't say 'out of qual' if she felt confident. Or would she? Then it pops up, one of those little intuitive itches, and the XO says, "Captain, ask her, can she see where the fog ends?"

He gives her a sharp, quick smile. "Look, Duck." He *would* call her Duck to make her feel more relaxed, make everybody feel more relaxed. "This fog came in awfully quick. Can you find a clear spot?"

"Roger, sir, elevating." A lighter tone. Firmer, higher pitch. She hadn't thought of looking for a clearing. She should have.

The captain's face seems calmer. He's almost smiling. "Ok, XO." The bridge watch takes a breath to hear him. "Are we forgetting anything?"

She ticks off her mental checklist. The phone talker has reported the ship at full power. The officer of the deck had already reported the flight deck manned to take the aircraft on board. All the emergency teams are on station. The ship is ready. The lost-bull lowing of the ship's foghorn seems forlorn, but as solid and comforting as ground.

The speaker squalls out Duck's voice, "This is Bumble Bee Two One. We got a clear patch of air. About five miles due north of your position…"

The captain raps out. "Spike, bring her to flank, best speed. Come to course zero zero zero." He turns to her. "How do you make it, XO?"

"I make it fifteen minutes we can get there. Thirty knots. In this visibility? Risky."

"Unstable weather like this, that hole will close."

"Worries me, though, Captain, this speed in the fog."

"Me too. Get down on the foc'sle. Get up in the eyes of the ship, up in the bow. Listen for anything. If you see anything, send up a conning order on your brick, I'll be right here with mine." The captain holds up his brick, a palm-sized interior communicator. "Conning Officer! Ensign Bailey! You stay next to me. Got it?"

"Aye-aye, sir," says Ensign Bailey as he is supposed to do.

Ensign Sean Bailey hates his life and he thinks, what's that supposed to mean, *stay next to me?*

Puking into a plastic bag for nearly a week had been bad enough, but even with the weather calmed, he hates his life. Four months out of Purdue, he should be in flight training right at this instant. But here he is, the most junior officer on the oldest, most fucked up ship he could imagine, and already a month of endless watchstanding, the ship beating the living shit out of him, one crashing wave after another, a set of binoculars like a brick on a string around his neck—and nobody seems to know what they were doing. This officer of the deck, his boss on watch, four-eyed *Spike*. More like stick-up-his-ass. The XO a bull-dike bitch, Mama-san. Voice like a bullfrog, butt like it, too. Or the skipper, his soft potbelly, some sort of goofy Ichabod Crane. What's all this sweat? He thought he'd be able to get a couple of cool spots up on Facebook, but even that was down hard, or turned off. No email even for the last six days.

You stay next to me?

Why? The door out to the bridge wing ought to be close enough. At least he'll be able to breathe there. Look at old Ichabod, wired so tight it's a wonder his ribs don't snap. Look at him, face buried in a radar repeater, literally scratching his ass. An hour ago, he'd been fast asleep in his chair. Fast the fuck asleep and the watch tiptoeing around like kids at Christmas.

Ensign Bailey slides over to the door, looks out on the bridge wing. He is the conning officer, isn't he? Shouldn't he be where he can see something, not that anyone can see anything in the fog? Fuck this.

They should have told him at Purdue they wouldn't let him fly. What good was any of this if they wouldn't let him fly? Kidney stones. Fucking kidney stones and you don't get to go to flight training, and now he's some kind of indentured servant working off his full ride through school on the deck of a fucking, ancient-ass, broke-dick destroyer. Screw it. Screw it. He can't wait to get off watch and get to the gym. Four years six months and a few days and he'll be out. Can't happen soon enough. Maybe Swann will be in the gym after she gets on deck. Being in a helo would be a fuck-load better than this. Especially with Swann. Calm. Sense of humor. Maybe a little old, but you had to admit, still a babe.

"Conning Officer! Come here. I said I wanted you right next to me." Ensign Bailey jumps. It isn't like the skipper to raise his voice. Then: *In the pilothouse. This is the captain speaking. I have the conn.* And this tells the ship that the captain alone, and not Ensign Bailey, would give helm orders. So why do they need him?

"Uh sir. Respectfully request permission to go below." The way Ensign Bailey sees it, there was no reason to stick around if he'd been relieved of the conn. He'd said 'respectfully request' so that meant the skipper was supposed to say something calming like, "It's ok, Ensign. You'll be fine, don't worry." He did not expect the skipper to say so murderously, "By all means. Right when things are a little tight. Abso-fucking-lutely go the fuck below. You are relieved of your duties. Officer of the Deck, get somebody up here right now. Get me a naval officer." The boy stands frozen in place. "Go. Get the fuck off my bridge. Don't come back. Do it."

The pilothouse goes dead quiet.

This had never happened before. Nobody liked Ensign Bailey and what he said was outrageous. Spike looks like he's going to commit murder—and the watch wishes the XO had not left the pilothouse.

The speaker sprays Swann's radio voice into the air. "Uhhhh Charlie Three Victor, this is Bumble Bee. We have a little unusual vibration up here. No chip light. No other indications, no unusual noise. But we need to get on deck. I'm falling in close astern of the ship. Uhhh, tell the captain I don't think this is serious. A little anomaly. But we're initiating the ditch checklist as a precaution."

The watch sees the captain bark into his brick, "XO, we've got to get the bird on deck. Do you see anything out there?"

At the eyes of the ship, the very tip of the bow, the XO leans out over the water and sees nothing. She cannot see the water below, cannot see the air above. But she can listen. She can hear. All the thump of the screws, the wash of the great intakes sucking air down into the ship's engines, all of it is muffled behind her.

She tells the captain, "No visibility. But I can't hear anything. We are going fuck-all quick, sir."

"What? We go slow and fail?"

"I didn't mean that, sir."

"Just. Keep on it, XO."

"Aye-aye, sir."

Beneath her, the ship quivers. This vibration, they must be near full speed. Banging along like this—hit some small craft, going this fast, the ship will chew it to pieces and spit it out through the screws. All week, she had dreaded some yahoo in a sailboat, plastic hull and narrow mast, no radar reflector, hard to see by eye even in clear weather. Near a strait like this, it could be anything. Fisherman with an outboard motor. Some kayaker adventuring north. Some fool is out here. Certainly. In the fog, you think you are alone. This weather lets you imagine yourself alone. Safe. Everything else hidden, inconsequential. But you are not alone. You are never alone.

And she is not alone. All the ship is behind her. She had been sent here to listen, to watch, the only set of ears and eyes with the experience; she was the one the captain trusted most. Proud of the danger and the thrill, she flies over the water, proud of her calm mind. She is proud of her careful, clear words, one spit out cleanly after another into the brick with her firm, command voice: "*Right—Full—Rudder. All Back Emergency Full. Boat in the water. Port bow.*"

Proud that she had seen it. Proud, but hoping to God she had been quick enough after she'd glimpsed, almost imagined, the dim white hull of something. Too close, the ship's bow first swings toward it. A cabin cruiser like a mirage crossing right to left. There are people topside, three of them. Men. Staring up, aching close. Now closer. She hears the ineffectual little squall of the boat's whistle thundered into oblivion by the whole bellow of her ship's horn, five short blasts, the signal for an emergency maneuver. Dear God. This once, let me get lucky. Dear God, help me to have given the right order. Dear God, don't let us hit them.

The cabin cruiser turns away from them, not even thirty feet long, barely twenty feet from them it starts to slip past, now down the port side. They had missed being cut in half, but the destroyer's stern is still swinging toward the boat like a gate. She orders, "*Shift your rudder.*" The boat disappears into the fog behind.

She feels the ship right itself, then tip the other direction, hard, and dip her toward the mist away from the boat she can no longer see. The screw thumps, cavitating in reverse. She leans over the bulkhead, stares astern, a pale cloak over everything. The engines' air intakes utter ever lower notes, catch a breath at the bottom, begin to howl up again. The ship slows and her nostrils sting from the cut of the engine's exhaust. Something inside the ship's hull falls. A bang, then a crash. All those sailors, all those two hundred on board, all of them caught like her in this extreme maneuver, this heavy lean, as if the ship would continue to roll over, press her down into the sea to crush them all. She sees nothing astern, and she is certain the little boat cruiser had been swallowed up.

The brick barks. "XO! Report!"

"Fucking little cabin pleasure craft. I heard the horn squeak. Barely saw it. It went astern. Captain." She took a breath. "I don't know if I shifted the rudder in time."

Silence.

The ship staggers upright. Now dead in the water.

Then the captain's voice, "XO. The after lookout saw it. Well astern. We missed it. Brace up. We still gotta get some clean air."

The deck under her feet shudders, the screws coming back up to speed. Again, she puts her face forward into the tentacles of fog around them. It seems to be less dense. dreamy, it lightens around her. Then, like a curtain dropping, she is above the fog and a painful sun makes it seem as though the ship has left the earth to skirt tops of a brilliant cloud cover.

"XO, I need you on the bridge."

A few months on a ship, and no matter how worn-out a storm makes you feel, you can still sling yourself up four ladders to a pilothouse without losing a breath. She finds the captain out in the sun of the bridge wing gripping a radio handset. Over the speaker, Lillian squawks, "No, sir, not getting worse. But it's persistent."

"Captain?" asks the XO.

"Vibration. Something wrong."

Aft, the sun catches the helicopter's cockpit glass to precisely illuminate two white helmets, tiny in the distance. Lillian and her nugget. The fog streaks up as if it might grip the helicopter, wrestle the two pilots and the one aircrew into the sea.

The captain stares astern and keys his microphone. "Bumblebee— Captain here. Can you make an approach with what you can see? Can you get over the flight deck?"

"Yes, sir. Request Green Deck."

"*Green Deck!*" the captain shouts, and Boatswain Pixie says, "Uh, Captain. The guys on the flight deck are still in the fog."

"The bird will blow it away when it gets over deck, get her on board. Do it."

Over the speaker, the XO hears the control tower—that aggravating, laconic pilot-talk, "Roger, Bumble Bee, I have you in sight. Not that I can see the flight deck. But the captain says you are cleared to make your approach. Green deck."

The aircraft picks its way forward toward the fortress of the ship's superstructure jutting up of the mist, the steel edges, so near those delicate blades beating a smooth thump. The blades whack as they cut air in the opposite direction to bring the bird over the flight deck. It hovers, wobbles. A little turbulence.

The cameras are too obscured to see the flight deck crew. But this is such a familiar moment—the XO feels them snaking up the recovery system to the aircraft, a heavy cable to attach to the aircraft's bottom to pull them down from the sky. There. It always surprises her to see how quickly the aircraft lands, drawn in with that cable.

The fog signal moans.

The captain steps back inside the pilothouse, climbs up onto his seat.

"Bumble Bee Two One is on deck," the phone talker announces. "Chocked and chained. Request permission to secure from flight quarters."

"All stop," the captain orders his ship. He lifts his hand, lets it fall into his lap. "Secure. XO, wrap it up for me, will you?

"Aye, aye, sir." All she has to do is let the ship go about its business. The crew knows what to do. This is routine. This is normal.

She steps up to the window next to her captain. The fog swells up around them, billows, and the world outside their pilothouse disappears until they are cocooned in the muffled swath of darkening haze, and the XO can tell it will be this way all night, maybe tomorrow, too.

She leans on the side of the captain's chair, feels the warmth of him, close and reassuring.

"OOD?" The captain raises his hand. "Have someone find Ensign Bailey and get him back up on watch. Tell him the captain will give him another chance."

He lowers his voice. "Always give them another chance, XO. Always."

"Bailey? What?"

"I'll tell you later."

She looks out into the blank haze. She had decided not to ask the question she'd had in mind, but something about forgiving Bailey for something she didn't know about, or perhaps the quiet reverence on the pilothouse tricks her and she says, "Captain. What if we'd hit that boat?"

Her captain closes his hand in a fist, bumps it lightly on the arm of the chair between each sentence: "We would have stopped. We would have used the helicopter to search. We would have put a boat in the water to recover the survivors. When the helicopter got too low on fuel, we would have maneuvered to take it on board. We would have written our reports, honestly and well."

These are the things he says, but both of them know there is no good answer. Someone—the ones in the boat, the ones in the helo, all of them—could have died.

"Captain? XO?" Lieutenant Swann brings in a clean air scent. "Good evening. sir. Ma'am. The aircraft is bedded down for the night." Opposite the XO, she leans against the high back of the captain's chair. She seems small, but she has the physical poise of a fine athlete. The XO says, "Lillian. Glad you could join us, girl."

"Wow. Pea Soup out there."

To the XO, Lillian sounds firm. Good. She got her shit gathered back together. This is the fucking ice-woman again. That's what you need in the cockpit, somebody with that kind of confidence. Born with it. Never had to earn it. A little stress and she had started to melt, the XO is sure of it. But she kept it together in the end. And a little luck. Born lucky. Christ, we were lucky.

The captain says, "Fine piece of piloting, Lillian. Fine airmanship."

"Thank you, sir." Her voice is as warm as the touch of the captain's arm—too warm, and this in itself makes the XO hesitate a moment. But that would have been the end to the XO's concern. She would have been content with the good luck of missing the cabin cruiser, getting Swann back on deck. All safe. But Swann says, "Great practice. My nugget sure earned his qual today. Vibration." She shakes her head. "Still don't know what it was. I should have put Bumble Bee on deck as soon as the fog set in."

The captain turns his head to the XO, stiffens and the XO knows he is struck mute. She says for him, "We almost hit a cabin cruiser. Lillian. You could have put the bird on deck? You let us do that—you let us run goddam thirty knots in the fog because you felt like it? Some whim so you could train your co-pilot?"

Swann shifts her feet, a little uncomfortable dance and the XO thinks, at least she feels it, a little sense of how close it had been. A little ashamed.

Swann says, "Well. Nobody gave *me* any report. How was I supposed to know?"

"You fucking mean to tell me…" The XO takes a breath to try to figure out how to end that sentence but before she can she realizes that Lillian had been scared shitless. That's what this is all about. Now she's trying to gaslight the whole thing? The captain lifts his hand. "Let it go, XO. It's water over the dam—Lillian, it was a little cabin cruiser. XO heard it from the bow. We never did up here. Little thing. We almost hit it."

Swann puts her hand on the chair's armrest, "Oh God," she sighs. Tired. "I didn't know. You should have said something, sir. I'm sorry." Her voice quavers a little.

The XO thinks, good, she's worried about the captain, what he will say about this, if he'll call for an investigation. She's earned a little worry about an investigation. She deserves a little goddam consequence.

Lillian lifts a perfect finger, the smallest movement. She touches the back of the captain's hand. Then, gently, the captain covers her hand with his, holds it, and returns her look.

Imagine never once in your life feeling pretty—the XO had never felt pretty. In all her life, she had never once been cute, or girly, or ever expected to feel that way. She had always wondered what it was like for these goddesses who walk the earth, their composure, their confidence that their very presence would do what Swann had done to the captain. She wished she could say something to him about it. But there are things people keep to themselves. There are things one never asks.

Before she left the bridge, the captain told her, and this was enough, "Great job XO. Great. You saved our asses today, Jennifer."

She dragged the pile of paperwork back to her stateroom across the passageway from the wardroom. By a trick of the ventilation, she can sometimes hear officers in the wardroom talk about her. She settled in to try to understand what she had to do for the institutional equipment next quarter. She heard it, then, Bailey talking, "Well, at least the Toad didn't try to bitch me out, I'da had to kiss her and turn her into a prince," and the junior officers squealed and giggled.

She didn't mind being called Mama-san all that much; there was a germ of affection in the words—so much better than Toad. Toad, she thought. She hadn't heard that one in years, and Jennifer found herself back on a school bus when she'd managed to get the seat in the rear corner where no one would pull her hair or whisper *Toad* into her ear. In front of her sat one of the boys in her class, a friendly boy. Nothing special. A regular boy. Next to him was one of the pretty girls. When the light began to dim on the long trip home, the girl had leaned over, placed her head on the boy's shoulder, and he tilted his head toward hers, put his hand over hers the same way the captain had done with Lillian. Jennifer remembers again how alone she had felt knowing she would never be that happy boy she had envied, that happy, happy boy with that pretty girl leaning up to him, that lovely girl's delicate body so comfortable and warm.

BILLY

THE WAY IT IS WITH OLIVIA, someone gets the blame. She's Catholic; blame seems a natural part of any untidy event. It's in her nature, find out who is at fault, then you'll know who needs absolution. That's all. They will be healed. The neighbor's poodle killed Billy, that seemed easy enough to me.

For Olivia, though, it isn't so easy, finding blame. There are always questions, reasons and disorder, acts of commission and omission. She is never so certain. She likes to search.

The way she saw it, you can't blame the dog. I see her point. The dog was big, the cat stupid. Just because the dog had a fancy haircut didn't mean he wasn't going to do what dogs do. He didn't have to consider, "Let's see, now, go about my business or chase the cat?" I'm sure he was a little surprised when he caught Billy. But I'm also sure he didn't have to mull it over, think something like, "Now what do I do? Maybe I'll give it a little tooth and see what happens."

I figure, the dog ran over, all billowy white and perky, gave Billy a shake and that was it. Except for the part where the cat finished himself off running with a broken back and cut throat. It was bad luck. No malice in it.

I didn't see any of this. Even if I had seen it, I'm pretty sure I wouldn't have been able to prevent it. These things happen quickly, you blink and it's over, a second of inattention and all you can do is pick up the pieces. Dogs are good at what they do. They're bred to it.

What happened, the cat went missing. He usually comes in at night. That Saturday he didn't return. He was a big cat, friendly. But like I say, he was stupid. We called him Billy after a general Olivia and I once worked for, also big, friendly and stupid.

At first Olivia wasn't all that concerned. He was gone, absent, doing things but coming back. Like me. Deployed. Away. And it isn't like she hasn't deployed a few times. Our rules: Don't die. Stay out of jail. Pay your bills.

Billy was gone. A fact of life. Late. At the worst, there was some little slip up. Like she said, we should have kept him in the house.

It would have been tough, though. The doors are always open out to the back. The sun warms up every day after it works through the Manassas haze you get in the developments as if the land can't forget it was a battlefield.

Billy liked to sit out in the garden, rest on raw dirt, put his nose up and breathe in that thick summer air tinged with the snappy smell tomatoes get in the sun. Hummingbirds would drop down a yard from his nose to talk about him, bitch him out. The birds looked interesting, maybe better than the canned stuff, so Billy took a crack at catching them. They were way too quick, too alert. Finally, he gave up. He would keep his head down on his paws, napping, ignoring those confounding birds.

That's the last time we saw him, sunning himself in the backyard while we went to Saturday vigil. No blame in that.

We like going to the Saturday evening vigil. It's never crowded, people we know fill the pews far enough apart to be comfortable, close enough to wave hello. Olivia and I are both usually wound down from the week so we can relax with each other. Often, she leans into me on the pew, puts her arm around me, holds me close to her. There is nothing that soothes me more completely. There, I'm calm with her soft scent and firm arm, oblivious to any liturgy. Me and Billy, basking.

Especially after returning from deployment, after months of noise on the ship or exhaustion, dirt, hunger in the field, I find myself astonished at her touch. There's no wonder in this. It's a hard life, but not like most people think. It isn't as if you spend day after day immersed in violence, one horrific assault after another. Nothing like that. And those things are generally not as bad as depicted.

For me, it's the anticipation that wears me out. Given long enough in work like ours, anyone will have a few moments, instances, to make you dread the next knock on your door. It always comes, that knock. It's never good news. They save the good news for staff meetings and commanders' conferences. Bad news comes to you fast, with the same grim report, the same terse words, it seems always at night.

With Olivia's arm around me, I let go. It's her acceptance, her warmth, her trust and the simple feeling she cares about me. To feel I've earned it, that care, and can collect. That's what I missed during all those deployments. That's what keeps me breathing sometimes from one moment to the next. She tells me, "You are a good man, Hank. You've done your duty. Now rest."

In the liturgy I say, "...I am not worthy to receive you. Only say the word and I shall be healed." Olivia believes that. She believes I deserve at least that.

I made a flyer with Billy's picture on it and started dropping them in mailboxes. I always liked that shot; Billy stares right at the camera and the light catches his eyes so you can see them yellow. He's sitting, his butt huge, head small and his face blank. It's an empty, confused look on a cat the color of a meatloaf.

The right kind of cat, you can say anything you want to it, call it names, malign its dignity, anything you want and you get the same I-know-nothing expression. They don't understand what's going on. They have a stupid trust that they are somehow above dramatic moments.

Truth is, they don't have to be that smart, nor do they have to know much of anything. Just enough to run away from a bounding dog. Just enough, like any ambush, the basic thing is to get off the spot. I thought Billy had at least that much sense, to get off the spot when he sees it coming.

The flyer said, "Billy. Nice but not bright. Missing since Saturday night." Then it gave our address and phone number. It said underneath, "Reward."

The old guy across the street was out letting his dog take its crap when I came by and I asked him if he'd seen our cat. He said no. Then he said that Maurice had a little tussle with a cat the evening before. Maurice was squatting a couple of yards away, the little balls on his trimmed ears dangling with his tongue as he shuddered that turd onto the common property and grinned at us.

I asked him if the cat looked like Billy and held up the flier and the neighbor said yes, he guessed that *was* the animal. Then I asked him where Billy had gone, and he pointed. I said thanks thinking he could have said something to me before; he could have followed the cat. I said thanks understanding how it feels when someone shows up to ask a question you never want asked. I didn't blame him. I said thanks thinking about Maurice eating, shitting and killing.

Creatures, all creatures, generally don't die right away. Most have minutes or hours or days where the machinery shuts down at some rate, more or less gradually, until it fails completely and everything is still. They hang on.

That's the uncomfortable part about learning to hunt or fish. You have to get used to ignoring that moment where the game isn't quite dead. The fair-minded will clock a caught fish on the head so it won't suffer too long. The hunting code I learned was you snap a pheasant's neck after the dog brings it up because most times, the shotgun isn't enough to kill it outright.

When you're teaching them how to hunt, the trick is teaching them to put their minds in another space during those moments. The first time a child threads a worm on a hook, you say, "Don't worry, the worm can't feel it." The first time a boy shoots a duck from the blind and the dog comes up, you praise his shooting, you exult. Kill your first deer and someone will blood you, maybe, wipe the blood from its cut throat on your cheek so you feel the joy of the moment. It doesn't take much, really, and you'll have them feeling nothing about it one way or another. They don't hear the deer sneeze blood, they don't see the bird rattle its wings inside the dog's mouth, they don't feel the worm wriggle in their fingers. Or, at least, seeing, hearing and feeling those things becomes inconsequential.

On the other side of it, medics talk about that golden hour, that period of time when it's still possible to arrest the dissolution, reach inside to patch the leak, immobilize the broken spine, repair the damage, let them live. Then it becomes consequential. Then the sights, sounds, smells and pulses are exquisitely vital.

The night Billy was killed, I thought I might have heard him. But I didn't go outside to look. The cat had this trick of climbing up on the neighbor's roof then demanding rescue. He would sometimes call to me from his perch in a tree, inside the garage, or under the car and I'd get up, pad around until I ferreted him out so he could lounge all over our bed, warm and safe. It was as if he would find a place where he depended upon me to come to him, pull him out as if it was some test of love.

I should have gone out to look, but I was too tired. I had some wine after mass then bourbon to keep the warm glow going. And I guess I was fed up with late night rescues. I'd been pretty sure I heard him, so I looked through the house, called for him.

At least I did that.

But I didn't get dressed, didn't go outside. He was a cat, a night animal, I told myself. He could take care of himself, and I rolled back into the rack and slept off my Saturday next to Olivia, breathing softly. I've learned that. You can't cup them in your hands every minute. You must let them do.

Then, Sunday morning, the old man tells me about his dog.

No answer when I called for Billy and no trace, no blood, no one had seen him, no sign he'd ever been out. I looked on Monday after Olivia went to work, called all the vets, all the animal hospitals, talked to the homeowners' association, banged on the neighbors' doors. I found out a lot. Like, the gardeners think they're getting paid too little. The one neighbor's wife had died and another's husband had left.

They found out a lot about me, too. By the time I was done, they knew Olivia had been promoted. A rising star. They knew I was on my way back to the Pentagon. They called me captain, but I say it's Hank now, and they nod, satisfied I'd made the shift. I told them I was taking a little break, a little time off. No responsibility, no worries for a bit. By the time I'd made it around the neighborhood, everyone knew I was happy. Everyone knew that when they asked, "So how are things going over there?" I could only shake my head and say I was glad to be out of it for a bit.

They all helped any way they could. But there was no sign of Billy, no golden hour to be found. All the while I thought about Billy bleeding out while I worked off the Jim Beam I'd had before bed.

The last couple years, I've had some pretty bad dreams, had trouble sleeping. Some of these stretch way back, surprising dreams from twenty-five years ago, back to my first days in the service. Over the years they'd go away then return like unwelcome relatives, knocking on the door out of nowhere. Usually not so bad I'd want help. When I start awake, Olivia reaches her soothing hand over to touch me, and we joke about it. She says, "Relatives?"

I'd say, "Worse, in-laws." And we'd roll over, sleep it off.

One of the old dreams snuck in when the cat went missing. It goes like this; I'm buried in earth wrapped in a wet sheet, twisted around my arms and between my legs, pulled over my head, over my eyes, over my nose. I'm breathing through my mouth, through a cardboard tube the size of a toilet paper tube, caught in the dirt, vertical over my lips. I can taste the dirt. Feel the wet sheet with the weight of the earth across my chest.

I don't know where I am. I don't know how deep the soil has been laid over me. I don't know why I'm there. I only know I'm buried.

It feels like I can move a little. I might be so shallow that all I have to do is push and I'll be able to sit up. Everything will be fine. But if I'm not shallow, if I lose control and start to struggle, I know that cardboard tube balanced over my lips will tilt away and I'll start to gag and panic with the dirt in my mouth until the wet sheet tightens over my nose, ears, legs, chest, balls, arms and I'll die like that. Trapped.

So do I wait, hope someone finds me? Or do I try to move, risk the tube falling away?

What I have to do—and the part that makes the nightmare so unbearable—I have to choke back the panic as long as I can, knowing, in the end, it will have me. It's not only being trapped. It's *knowing* I'm trapped, knowing I can choose. If only I can maintain control over myself.

I'm sure Billy had no such thoughts when the dog got him. A wounded animal has no responsibility to keep its wits. It only knows to fight back, run. A wounded animal abandons itself to fear and violence.

I suppose that's what the gardener found when he came across Billy, a vicious cat, crazed and wounded. I don't blame him for using his shovel. These are simple men, these gardeners. They come from the places where you still throw a litter of kittens in a gunnysack and pitch them into a pond because you have no use for them. You find a vicious animal, bloody, hissing and clawing at you under a bush and you use the point of your shovel to take off its head. Then you put it in a plastic bag and throw it in a dumpster. When somebody like me comes around waving a twenty-dollar bill, you go get the cat out of the dumpster and bring it to the guy, get your reward.

I don't blame him. How can you blame him for doing what he does? All he saw was a feral animal, vicious, probably diseased, big and threatening, begging for extermination. I paid him, asked him to take the cat away.

After we found out what happened to Billy, Olivia blamed the old man. There are lots of old men like him in this neighborhood. Most of these guys bought these houses when they were new in the 70's. The ones who are still here are the ones who never stepped up. They all look the same: some grey hair whipped over the crown. The same pained, shuffling gait. If not using a walker or a cane, they practice how to bend over. Oddly enough, they have wives with different sizes, shapes, colors and dispositions. But these guys, they are all the same, all sour.

I didn't blame him. Maurice wasn't his idea. He didn't want to get up every evening and let that bouncy, youthful and plain *big* animal yank on a leash, trying to make him fall over. He hadn't expected to feel achy and cranky. He hadn't decided to take on the dog. He had been doing the best he could, and the dog ran out day after day and crapped without anything happening at all until Billy, confounded by hummingbirds, blundered into becoming prey.

I don't see it as his fault. Shit happens. Like age. Like the inevitable cane or walker.

Olivia wanted to have the animal control guys come take the dog. "Vicious dog he can't control," She said, "Who knows what would have happened if Billy had been someone's child?"

Dogs like that, I told her, they are not wired to kill children. Only cats and other small animals, I told her that it's only natural selection.

I didn't tell Olivia about opening up the garbage bag with Billy stiff and soiled, stinking the way dead animals do, blood, shit stained. I told her the gardeners had found him and he was dead. No sense giving her all the details like the way his eyes were closed, not staring, and how odd it looked with his fur and limbs stiff and twisted by the spade or the garbage where he was buried, who knows which?

That's what you get when something is dead. After that in between moment, the period while it's dying, it goes completely limp and it falls, all the joints twist into inappropriate positions. It's no wonder we can't help ourselves from cleansing the dead, straightening them, placing them in positions we recognize. Whenever there was an IED or bomb or blunder, after we got the wounded to their golden hours, people would straighten the dead. Line them up, retrieve pieces of them and place the parts under sheets to make it look like they were whole. Put children next to their parents, husbands near their wives. Anything to make it seem less random while the dead waited to be taken away. As if they waited for anything. As if they had anything left to wait for while we waited, tasting the copper dirt, until we could go on to the next moment, then the next, then the next, imagining what it would be like to be them.

These things happen quickly, you blink and it's over. A second of inattention, a few minutes of chaos, then nothing but leftover time. And all you can do is get everybody focused to pick up the pieces. The trick is, teaching them to put their minds in another space during those moments. You deal with it matter-of-factly, and these *things*: supine, limp, straightened out—these are not the ones you knew. These are only the shells of a once living being. Now it does not live. They were confounded and blundered into becoming prey. There is no blaming it for its death.

And who do you find to blame? Where are the ones at fault? They *believe*, those who come with the bomb strapped to their chests or driving that car or taping that cell phone to the shell. They see only a feral animal, vicious, diseased, big and threatening. They see evil. They see the devil in it, begging for extermination. Blame seems pointless. I tell you, we were not seeking vengeance, only solutions.

When you put a guy up on a water board, it used to be they didn't know what was going to happen. There's no surprise about it anymore. And nobody does it anymore. We know better. A pack of cigarettes and beer. That's what people say works better.

Once, it had been a novelty, close held, that waterboard. Years ago, young and full of piss, I had known it was possible. In training, they told us what was going to happen, but I couldn't believe they would do it. But it was training, good training. The other guys would stand in ranks being screamed at and pushed by the make-believe guards as the instructors put an officer up for everyone to watch. They were careful, a doctor standing by, a shrink. At first you try to hold your breath but the sheet over your face seems to tighten up, mashing in your nose and your arms and legs are caught immobile. All you can do is try not to move, because if you do, you might slip away from being able to actually take in a breath. Then you gag. And you can't keep control anymore. You lose your wits. You thrash. You scream, puke and aspirate water. They lift the board up at the feet with your head down so they can control it. The doctor and the shrink keep their eye on you and to make sure it doesn't get out of hand. They let me lose hope before they dug me out.

Everybody knows about that now. Everybody has seen it on TV.

They taught me. They told me there's no shame in all that. They told us it's training. There's no blame in it.

The rule for captivity used to be survival with honor. I don't know what the rule is anymore. Don't die. I guess. Stay out of jail.

I don't know what anyone else got out of watching me gag and thrash. Nobody wanted to talk to me about it. Ever. And I didn't talk to anyone who'd watched. What I got out of it was I never wanted to be prey. Ever.

What happened to Billy? He was out of his element. When we got him from the shelter, they told us he'd grown up in an apartment, never went out. We took him in; he stepped up. He got our garden where he could pee on the plants, the lawn where he could roll around picking up fleas in the summer and the porch where the hummingbirds came down whenever they were bored to bitch him out. He was happy, but clueless. Always bewildered and dumb.

Olivia said, "So we blame the cat?"

But the cat can't be blamed either. He was an accident waiting to happen. Didn't know about hummingbirds, didn't know about poodles.

The guy we put up on the board was out of his element. He didn't know about these people who had him. He didn't know what was going to happen. What they told me, they were only going to give him a little tooth and see what happened. I said okay. You can't cup them in your hands every minute. You must let them do.

The way we put it, we were looking for reason, some hysterical twitch of truth. But watching the film, you see prey at that moment before passing from life. A creature, in between, not knowing whether or not he should try to sit up.

And I could see it was us—we who had been taught the trick of feeling its life in our fingers. The worm's twitch? Inconsequential.

Olivia is as Catholic as a human being can be. Whenever she looked in a mirror, she saw a Catholic girl then, a Catholic woman now and a Catholic eternity. And I was Catholic with her.

I don't ask her to change. I don't blame her. I am not worthy to receive you, but only say the word and I shall be healed, I pray.

I pray the rosary, take a lap around the beads daily. I say "Hail Mary, full of grace." I say, "Pray for us sinners now and at the hour of our death, Amen." When Olivia puts her arm around me, I feel comforted. I think it's possible I have erred. It's possible I am forgiven.

But at night they come with the wet sheet and I balance this cardboard tube over my mouth. If I move, it may fall away. I grip back my panic, knowing that sooner or later I will not be able to keep it inside, it will spill out. No saving spade will slice down to end it. No careful arm over my shoulder will pull me closer ever again.

Olivia fixes blame. It's in her nature. She is not to blame. She has found her absolution; she knows who is to blame. They are. Those others. I don't tell her everything. Some things, I don't trust her to know.

But someday, soon, they will ask. There will be questions. They'll show me a picture then have more questions about reason and disorder, acts of commission and omission. There will be blame. I do not believe there will be a comforting arm around my shoulder.

Or, perhaps, no one will come. Perhaps there will be no such question, no search for blame, no search for any sort of truth in the noise of speculation and headlines. Life for me will go on as it is. Me basking, pretending there's solace, ignoring those confounding birds.

Either way—this is the point—I cannot bring myself to sit up, not knowing how deep it is above me. So I wait, out of my element, at that in-between moment with no golden hour.

And no one will say the word.

And I will not be healed. This I know.

Ever.

RANDY ROOT

THE SUNDAY MUTTER of distant afternoon traffic joined the breeze from the garden below and woke her. She rolled toward him, wrapped herself in the cool sheets and put her hand on his chest to feel it rise and fall, rise and fall.

"What?" he murmured out of a doze.

"Nothing. I wanted to touch you. I'm thinking, I might as well get the most out of this."

"This what?" His eyes were still closed, his words half-whispered. Yes, what is this? she thought. This pause, this *afterlife*, some sort of license to enjoy—what? The smugness of good sex. That's enough, maybe. Nobody had made any promises. "I don't know. Hank. This moment. Right now."

"Hmm." He opened his eyes, stared up as if fielding an answer during a conference, the two of them in yet another conference room with all the faces turned to him, waiting. And he glanced at her, the same budget-markup-look of anticipation, wariness, and threat he would give her during testimony or briefings—calm, serpentine, the way he would deflect a question to her. She almost expected him to say, "I'll let Mary answer that—Mary?"

He let out his breath. Eyes, grey-blue. She had never known their color before. And they were not reptilian. Maybe like a bird, a raptor. But now different. He put both hands over hers, completely relaxed. A dozen years together in the Pentagon, he'd never been like this, gentle and calm. The moment they had met for lunch, he'd been different. Everything had been different. When she saw his name on the list of speakers for their conference, she had looked forward to seeing him, old friends. Colleagues. But this? She had never imagined finding themselves here, a weekend in her stowaway apartment. Had either of them ever wanted this when she had worked for him? Maybe she had. Sometimes a little. On the road once or twice maybe they'd had a bit much to drink. But in those days she had a splendid husband to occupy her. What was this, the lack of spouses? Both of them, different and more grown together in some way. And he *was* different, or maybe this part of Hank was the one he never showed anyone, the Hank who knew how to relax, breath easily, the Hank who didn't measure every word. "Here's what I've always wondered." She pulled her hand out from under his, sat up with the sheet wrapped around. "Why do you call yourself Hank? Does everyone still call you Hammering Hank? You know, you should use your real name instead of 'Hank.' Hayden is a better name for you. Everyone knew you were a hard ass. Why not use Hayden? Classier name. I always wondered."

"Hammerin' Hayden?"

"No. Ha! But no, I meant—look. When we worked together, I never thought you were kind. But you are. Gentle, too. And when I think back on it, you did kind things for people all the time. I bet you're even kind to your wife."

"Former wife."

"See? Anyone else would have said 'my ex,' or 'practice wife.' You say 'former.' You are a kind man, a Hayden. Not really a Hammering Hank."

"I always liked Olivia. I never had anything against her."

"That's what I mean. You defend her even now for leaving you. You are a kind, kind person, Hank. Why not Hayden?"

"Hayden." He snorted and spoke to the ceiling. "Hayden. I never liked Hayden. My dad made me use it. I was Hayden Bell the Fourth. But my version of Hayden was a fuck-up. Fucked up college so he couldn't get into a good law school. Fucked up and got drafted. Whenever my dad said 'Hayden' I'd cringe. Anything but Hayden—the name of some alumni club chairman."

He'd definitely been Hank. Working first for him, then *with* him when he'd moved up and he let her take over. Sharp, tough, capable. Maybe that's what divorce does to some men, makes them accessible. Her divorce had certainly made her more accessible. At least changed. So why did she feel so guilty? What was there to feel guilty about?

"I've been thinking about this, Haydon, now that you're out and officially political. A cheesy government service staffer can be Hank. But a Deputy Assistant Secretary of Defense needs to be Hayden Bell the Fourth. Hey! Wait! This is scandalville. Does all this mean I'll be the secret girlfriend of a DASD?" She said it, 'DazDee.'

"I always thought it sounded like a disease."

"It is. Oh, we simply *must* see each other again after the hearings, or better, after you get confirmed. I *so* want to be fucked by a DASD."

"As if you haven't been already." And they both laughed. All those stumbling congressional staffers they had seen boosted up to suddenly become a Deputy Assistant Secretary. Shiny. New. Dying to poke a stick in the eye of some Pentagon drone and then, when things get so bad no one else will take the appointments, the non-pols take over for a while. Hank would bring a lot to it, all those years of experience, that confidence. Risky, taking those jobs. You can't become un-political once you become someone's appointee only to find yourself forever tainted with the tail end of a failing administration. And this one was certainly failing after six years of war in two countries. She felt so remarkably comfortable with him.

"So…Hayden. When did you decide to make the change?"

"SecDef asked, I said okay. Good lead into retirement so I can get one of those fellowship gigs like you, get out of that rat hole."

"No. The name. When did you start calling yourself Hank?"

"Oh. That. Boot camp. I get to boot camp and there I tell them I'm Hank, like a cowboy or a fireman. No more Hayden. And presto—Hayden is only a memory."

He went still. Quiet. Almost as if he'd stopped breathing. This is when they go into that cave they're always talking about. Fade away into some thought they never let out of their minds. She'd had him talking for a bit. What did she have to lose now? Why not prod him? He had once seemed so much older than her. But the fifteen years between them didn't seem like much anymore. They had converged, somehow, found a shared place on the bed. Something like a relief. Another surprise.

"So now." She poked him in the ribs. She liked the hard little pieces of him there. "You tell me your story. Then I'll tell you mine. Ok?" She poked him again, harder.

"Ouch... damn! *Will* you quit that..."

"Boot camp. Tell me about boot camp. Changing your name. It seems weird, you know? Wasn't your daddy rich and your momma good looking?" Joke with them. She'd learned that. They tell you things when you get them laughing.

"Well. Sure. Look. Here's a thing about young men, this thing in all of them that makes them try on different costumes to figure out who they are."

"Like I don't know that. I remember being seventeen. I remember dating. I was married to a young man, once, remember?" She poked him again. "Let's get something to eat. Let's get some wine." She swung her legs up out of the sheet, ripped it off him, dropped it on the floor. "Come on, Boot, time to get moving."

He laughed, "Hey! Isn't it supposed to be me who wants to jump out of the rack after insemination? Aren't you supposed to want to lie around and let those little guys do their work?"

"Equal opportunity. No fucking glass ceilings here. Get up." She tumbled into her tights, threw his t-shirt over her head.

"Mine!"

"Not anymore. Hey. Only button that shirt half-way. I want to get my money's worth out of this."

The kitchen. Sweet olives she loved. Cold chalky wine. He drew the cork. She took down the glasses.

And all of it felt a little false.

It seemed as though they were in a play, acting, a preview before opening night. Even this talk about boot camp. His name. He'd never change his name, she was certain. Playacting. Truly. Or maybe play, she thought. Why not? Why not play.

She touched his glass with hers. "Explain. Boot camp. Boys will be boys. Trying on costumes. Y-M-C-A!" she sang. "Y-M-C-A, Young men…. Truth or dare. Tell the truth, now. All the truth." He was truly having a good time. Nothing fake about that smile. She chuckled him outside to the table in the shade of the garden, the sun now slanting toward dusk.

"Drink wine. Tell the truth," she said. "Do you swear to tell the whole truth, and nothing…"

"Oh God. Boot camp was open season on the truth. See, nobody knows you. That's the secret of it. You start all over, clean slate. You could say whatever you wanted about yourself, and we made it up as fast as we could. Remember the movie *Little Big Man*?"

She nodded, "Dustin Hoffman."

"*Little Big Man* made it cool to be a Native American. At least three or four guys in boot camp had mothers who were Indian Princesses, always Cherokee. A couple of guys had fought Golden Gloves. We had race car drivers. Whatever."

"Like I said, you should try dating. Same thing." She waved her hand. "The lies you hear when you're a girl." She shook her hair down over her eyes, flipped it back over her head.

He held up his hand. She'd expected him to laugh. But he said, "You're beautiful. It's true. More so now than when you were twenty-five."

Those greying eyes, the fading sunlight bringing out flecks of warm brown. She said, "I was different, then, that's all." She reached across the table. Their fingertips touched. "Senator Stenburg thought I was pretty hot."

"Stenburg. Hell. Give yourself some credit. He thought Mrs. Bush was hot. No, Mary, you were stunning then. You are now. I could take you anywhere."

She lifted her hand away. Where would he take her? What plans did he have? She didn't want to hear any more about men making plans for her. Why always that? "Enough. Stop it, Hank. Tell me more about boot camp."

He drank his wine, considering. Blinked his eyes. Shut them. He'd heard the sharpness in her voice. She would need to watch that. She softened it to say, "Really, go on, Hank. Sorry I got a little snappy. You got drafted into the Navy."

He narrowed his eyes at her. "No. Volunteered. But look. I hadn't planned any of it. I didn't come from that kind of family. And I didn't have much choice. What you don't know—you got into the Navy because you didn't want to get drafted and wind up in the Army or Marine Corps with the guys who were going to lose the Vietnam War. And who wants to be a loser at twenty? Boys, all boys—all they want to do is win and get laid like they do in the movies. The only problem was, when you enlisted in the Navy you had to give them four years. The draft only wanted two. So you were stuck. Four years washing dishes and painting bulkheads, or two years shooting people, or jail, or Canada. Pick one."

Bitter. What was this? It made her nervous. Hurt? "Hey." She reached for him again. "Hey. It's a long time ago. It worked out."

"You're right." He blew out a breath. "I didn't mean to get worked up."

He looked out over the garden, his face firming up again. He had somehow aged to become more handsome. The sun had slid over the tops of the trees, slipping lower, edging it under the awning. He looked a little embarrassed, self-conscious or something. She slid her chair over next to him, took his hand.

"Hayden." She rubbed the top of his hand with her thumb. "You better be ready for me to call you Hayden forever, now."

"Damn. Nearly forty years." He smiled looking at the last glow of the sun in the trees, drifting away again. To pull him back she said, "Tell me about the hazing in boot camp. Wasn't it awful with all that hazing?"

"No. No hazing. They didn't even call it boot camp. Recruit training, that's what we called it. We had a drill instructor, kind of. This little Puerto Rican guy, Dominguez. When we get off the bus, we expected him to go into one of those screaming tirades everyone has seen on TV. You know, the one where he yells, 'I am not your mother, I am not your daddy,' until he gets to the punch line: *for the next eleven weeks, I am your God on earth, forget all the rest of your gods.*"

"He didn't do that?"

"No." Hayden had emptied his glass. She reached over with the bottle and he let her pour. "First thing he tells us—" he mimicked a Puerto Rican accent. "—I am your Recruit Company Commander. If you want a drill instructor, you have to go see the Marines on the other side of the fence or you can go join the Army.'"

"I didn't know you did voices."

"Not exactly a PC climate in those days." He'd come out of the cave. Amused. "But we were tolerant. Dominguez—he made us tolerant of each other. He stands up in front of us and in the same nice, calm voice, he says, 'Please address me as Petty Officer Dominguez.' He says, 'Until you finish recruit training, you will call me 'sir' for practice. Afterwards, later, you will use the word 'sir' for officers only because you will be a Sailor, like me, and officers are our leaders.'"

"Christ. You remember every word."

"I kept expecting some very bad guys to show up, start the real boot camp, the one with yelling for no reason, calling us worms, making us drop and give them twenty."

He looked down into his glass. "But it didn't happen. He lined us up in ranks the first time, all of us trembling, our collars itching with the new haircuts, Dominguez points to his hat, that white sailor hat, and says, 'the first thing we do, is we earn the right to wear this white hat.'

"We didn't give a damn. That little white dixie cup looked stupid to every single one of us. I mean, it was the sort of hat mothers used to put over kids heads in the sun. But Dominguez treats it like it's a crown. He's got it all cocked to one side, curled at the edges, and he says we have to pass the first part of the course, and either we all put on our white hats together or no one ever wears it."

She realized she had disappeared. There was no other audience other than her, but she had grown invisible in the dark beyond the last of the setting sun's proscenium, the actor now completely still and quiet, his wine glass tilted in his hand. She had been forgotten. Too much like her husband, all those others, cutting her out like this when they think she's said something wrong. Her husband had kept dropping her from his conversation until he faded away, leaving her near forty without even a child, only a thank-you-ma'am-for-your-labor, think-tank fellowship. You take them to bed and they revert. What gives them the right to be themselves after you fuck them? She put down her wine, crossed her arms over her belly. How to get him out the door. "So. It sounds like a lot of fun, boot camp."

Hank finally looked at her. She could tell he'd caught the edge to her voice. Fuck it. Let him clam up, be mad. But he said, "You don't want to hear the story anymore?"

"Oh? How can you tell? What is this, another bullet in the head, *Full Metal Jacket* story?" This had all gone so wrong. Now she couldn't get that comfortable feeling back. He is Hayden, accept him as Hayden. Don't get confused. But she was confused. This was an overreaction.

He muttered, "Maybe I should go."

"Go? So soon? What a surprise." She tried a smile. "Sure. Go. If you want. No harm. Don't forget your shoes. I've got to pee."

Get up out of a chair. Move around. Get away for a bit. Take your time. The whole thing seemed nuts anyway. A little roll in the hay, a little healthy exercise, that's all. But this lovely, smooth, *caring* lovemaking in her apartment with birds chirping like idiots outside. The garden had rumpled the bedroom air with its scented fingers over them, a Sunday afternoon, neither of them drunk, not in the dark. But open in the bright air of her bright room, everything seen, tasted and worshipped. They'd worshipped what? And now the day finishing. What had it been for a moment?

Transcendence was the word she found. They'd worshipped transcendence, slipping away as if drugged, losing all the errors of her marriage and life. Him, too, obviously. Now remembering, going back in time. Boot camp. Had she made him so comfortable? Had she done that to him in bed? Like some courtesan geisha now listening to him confess his life? Now she's nearly thrown him out, over what? She could barely remember why. Oh yes, she'd seen it. He'd already abandoned her.

She washed her face. She dried herself with the hand towel, breathed in its clean scent. Waited longer. She would go back out and the table would be empty. He would have taken her at her word. Run out. A coward.

But no one would call Hank a coward. His shoes were still next to the bed. And there he was. "I opened the bottle I brought with me." He pointed at her glass, rich deep red. He'd lit the oil lamp and a couple of candles on the table.

She moved close enough to lean on the edge of his chair seat, press against his shoulder. "I thought you might have left."

"Should I?" He reached up, took her hand.

She turned his hand palm down. Gripping hard. She shook it like she would a naughty child's hand. "I don't think so. Hayden. Not yet. It's been too nice a day and I don't want all this to finish on a sour note. Do you? No. Of course not." She pulled him up. "Come sit with me, let's neck a little or something."

She took him over to the outdoor couch she kept out on the brick patio where she often sat alone to watch the candles on her table and see the lights inside her apartment after dark the way neighbors looking in might see them. She liked the warm, warm touch of the arm he placed around her. She hoisted her feet up on the couch, leaned her back onto him.

She said, "I think we'll call you Hank. I think I like you tough. Go on. Tell me the story. You're the one with the early morning flight. I have plenty of time. You can stay if you want."

"This is pretty dull."

"Isn't that what people do, pay attention to each other's dull stories?"

He leaned over, kissed her forehead. "Yes, they do. They sure do. Here's the dull part; boot camp is fine. All organized. All predictable. Everything is alphabetical and by the numbers. I get the top bunk, but under me, it's empty. Everybody else has a rack-mate. It goes like that for a week. And you don't want to stick out in situations like that. Something about that sort of atmosphere makes you want to be like everybody else. Less chance to be observed if you fuck up, I guess. Finally, after a week of sweating over this, we come back from chow and I get one, a rack-mate."

She poked him, "I get it. This is some weird boys-on-boys coming out story, right? Rack-mates? Hank, now you tell me you're *gay*? So maybe you ought to come out before the hearings?"

"You say that? After all we've been through?"

It made her laugh.

"No. Nothing so interesting. This guy wasn't gay. He was what we called a 'holdback,' a guy who flunked out of boot camp. They'd kicked him out of whatever holding cell they had him in to rejoin the training. Neat, though. Squared away. He had this absolutely level crew cut with one of those cowlicks in front making his hair go backward where most people have a part. I found him when we got back from lunch kneeling in front of his rack. I thought we'd caught him praying."

Hank was slipping away again. But intent this time. Concentrating, not like leaving her, he talked faster as if he wanted to get it out. "Lots of guys prayed. Even I prayed. But this guy was folding his t-shirts. Only, very slowly and very, very carefully, making it perfect. He looked like he'd been some sort of accident victim the way he folded his shirts. I thought to myself, he's scared. He's making sure there are *no more mistakes.*

"Mistakes? What mistakes?"

"I give this guy my friendliest, 'How-you-doing? I'm Hank.' I held out my hand and that's when he stands up and says, 'I'm Randy Root, Seaman Recruit.'"

"Randy Root?"

"Honest to God, Randy Root. When he says this, it's funny. I'm about ready to laugh. He's putting me on. But there was something wrong. So I didn't. I shook his hand and said, 'Hi, I'm Bell.'"

"What was it? What was wrong?"

"You know how it is when someone says something like, 'I'm very pleased to meet you.' and you're sure it's exactly the same way his mother taught him to do it? Randy says that to me and his eyes are friendly but very wary, hurt sort of. I know right then someone taught him to say, 'I'm Randy Root, Seaman Recruit,' because they'd thought it might be funny. Randy thought it was okay people laughed. Even if he couldn't figure out why they were having so much fun."

"Forrest Gump."

"No. About Forrest, he was never confused. But Randy was confused about everything except for that very specific set of skills they'd taught him. Fold his shirts. Make his bed. Line up in ranks. Hold his hand stiff to salute. Believe me, I didn't want to, but after thinking about that rack empty for a week, I was pretty sure I'd been designated as the guy who had to get Randy through boot camp."

"But how come? How did he get into the Navy? How did he pass the test?" She sat up. "He couldn't do it. You failed to keep him in." What was it that had so fixed this story in him, almost forty years ago?

"Exactly the opposite. Randy was a savant, dead-on perfect in everything."

"A boot camp savant! Randy Root! Oh you have to be making this up. This is Forrest Gump.

Hayden held up an open hand. "I swear. All of this is true, at least as well as I can remember. Really. Someone had spent a lot of time teaching Randy how to fold clothes, march in step, put away his tray after meals. He fit right in and he had become good at it. He had a good way of picking up other guy's mistakes, not going "Gotcha!" like some of the other guys, but saying, "Maybe we better look at that buckle again," using the same words every time, the same way he'd been taught to say 'Randy Root, Seaman Recruit.' I mean, somebody, I'm dead certain, had to teach him step-by-step how to tie his shoes and he did it the same way every time. Perfectly. And we were clueless. Everybody went to him for help. He had that stuff down cold."

She twisted her legs up on the couch, rolled over onto her back so she could look up at him with her head in his lap, took his hand in both of hers to hold it on her chest. The warm glow of the apartment's lights made his face softer, less angled. Older. "Tell me more."

"There's plenty. Here's the thing, Randy wanted to be a Sailor. Nobody else did. But Randy did. I don't think he understood that he would be drafted into Army if he wasn't in the Navy. It didn't seem to make any difference. He loved the chow, loved folding his clothes, loved having all these guys around who were his friends. And we *were* his friends. Nobody ever called him Randy Root, Seaman Recruit. Nobody wanted to make fun of him because he was a little slow. Hell, we were all a little slow. We all felt stupid trying to fold clothes and learn the difference between port and starboard, stay in step. All Root wanted was to belong. Pretty soon, I guess it's what boot camp does, we *all* wanted to belong."

She could feel him breathing, evenly, tightening his thighs, his abdomen.

"Go on," she said.

He started again, now firmly Hammerin' Hank, the biting, ass-chewing tone. "Better yet. I was beginning to feel pretty good about all of this, got some things that never left me. Boot camp turned out to be pretty good. Because it worked out, like a name change. I could do fine in the Navy. After all that time—college, home, high school, fucking kindergarten—spending all that time 'not up to the task,' as my dad put it. Finally. I *was* up to the task. I hadn't known how bright I could be. I hadn't known I was strong or capable; I got an 'excellent' on every test and inspection and the others, the other guys in the company, they all watched how things worked with Randy and me, and they looked up to me. To us. None of it because of my dad or anything else. Remember the white hat? When we got to change the hats?"

"Sure."

"After five weeks, all we wanted in life was to be able to wear that silly looking dixie cup. It was like the plain girl on the first day of class. By the fifth week, she's gorgeous. We wanted that hat curled on the edges, cocked over our eyes, the same way Dominguez cocked it. And the day finally comes. All we had to do was spend the day packing our sea bags, get ready to march across a bridge over the old San Diego River to the new barracks, where everybody wore dixie cups and the real training would begin, and as far as I was concerned, I wasn't going to be Hayden ever again. I didn't think I'd be in the Navy long, but I knew it was going to work out great, and I'd be Hank. I'd be the guy they always say about, 'Oh *that* guy, I know about him' and it would be me, not my dad they talked about."

She straightened up. Stretched, leaned away into the big arm of the couch. "And look what happened. Now, you *are* that guy. Hayden Bell the Fourth, Deputy Assistant Secretary of Defense. Or almost. A senatorial inquest away. So. I get this. So who is Randy Root, who did he become?"

This made him still. He watched her face, his eyes dark in the last of the light. The candles streamed straight up, the traffic burped, some truck or something gearing up.

"They threw him out, didn't they?"

Hank looked away. "Dominguez calls me up to his office with Root. Root is nervous. But I tell him not to worry, it's okay. I don't remember the sound of Randy's voice. He didn't talk much. He did things. He was happy. Dominquez tells us, 'At ease,' because naturally, we report at attention, the way he'd taught us. Root stays at attention. He's that sort, tight, scared of the boss. How can you blame him? Guys like Dominguez, these were the guys who taught him how to do things when they held him back the first time, and we all knew it didn't go easy, that learning.

"I give Root a little nudge. He looks up at me. He relaxes, Smiles. I'm his pal.

"Dominguez says to me, 'How much do you help him with folding his clothes?'

"Neither Root nor I can say anything. Even today, I still want to think I was surprised. He goes to Root, 'Seaman Recruit Root.' See how funny that sounds? Root starts that stupid smile. He thinks it's supposed to be funny.

"Dominguez says, 'Does Bell help you make your rack? Does he fold your clothes?'

"Root gives him a big grin. He's relieved it's an easy question. He says, 'Sure.' He says I help him plenty.

"Dominguez dismisses Root. Tells me to stay, starts right in telling me to apply for OCS. He says he's going to get the CO to recommend me. He says he would be proud to serve under me if I became an officer. He says nothing is more precious than the people who will help out a shipmate.

"The last I saw Randy, he was on a bus, sitting near the window as we marched past. The bus was full of guys. Holdbacks, I guess. He waved at me. He smiled. But he wasn't part of the company anymore. We were marching. We couldn't wave back."

He stopped. She wondered if that was it: they couldn't wave back. Surely there was something else.

"You should have seen Root on that bus, Mary. He gives us a little smile and a wave. He wanted somebody to tell him he was doing good. Like any of us wanted. Like I wanted."

She wanted to feel him again, lean against him. His skin warm under his shirt. "I hid your shoes under the bed."

"I could have said something to Dominguez, talked him out of it. But I didn't. I let him go. Dominguez to this day, I bet, still thinks I folded Randy's clothes for him."

"So. What happened? He was drafted. Was he killed? Wounded?"

"Where did you say my shoes were? I better start getting out of here, or I'll be in a panic in the morning." He slid himself from her. Stood. "And I don't know. Hell, I don't know if he ever actually went in the Army. Never saw Randy Root, Seaman Recruit ever again."

All right then. Time for him to flee. Let him go. "Hank. That's it then. Everything worked out fine. Maybe you even saved him? Maybe he would have been killed in the Navy if he'd gotten in."

"Maybe."

She picked up the wine bottle, the bowl where there had been olives. He said the usual sorts of things men say when they've decided to leave. "Here, let me help. What can I carry in?" The traffic was louder now, the highway over the hill above them spilling over its noise, all the weekend escapees returning to the city, ending their Sunday jammed together on the road. This wasn't the end of it, though. What was she missing in all this? The candles were still going nicely. She couldn't reach what it might be.

He followed her into the kitchen, so she said to the sink, "Hank. It doesn't make you bad. That thing. That doesn't make you any less after all this time. So you took some credit you didn't deserve. You were young."

"I was. We were all young, away from home the first time—our first opportunity to be ourselves."

She washed the glasses, let him wipe.

"Your shoes. They're probably under the bed. Where I slipped them. Like I said."

For a moment, she thought he would stay. For a moment she thought the shoes were enough of a hint. But a breath later, they were in the elevator, her arm in his. At the front door, she stopped him to kiss him. He lingered long enough for her to hope.

"Forgive me, Mary." He gripped her, squeezing too hard. Strong. His arms high across her back. "I didn't plan this, I didn't even think it would go like this when you asked me to come over. And I sure as hell don't deserve it. But I'm awfully glad." The arms loosened.

She kissed him again. Reached up to hold his face. "Did you look for me? Did you hope to see me when you came here?"

"You know I did."

It seemed true. But she said, "That's not an answer, Hank. You taught me that, remember? Slipping off the answer you don't want to give."

He pecked her on the lips. "Yes. I came here for you. All of you. Every inch."

Good enough. She held him with both hands at his elbows, not letting him turn away. It felt domestic. It felt like the end of a Sunday like any other. Then he leaned his head over her shoulder and whispered, "Don't disappear." He took a breath, considering. "We deserve to have a lifetime of Sunday's like this, you and I."

She smiled up him, tried to lighten it up even though she felt a thrill as he said it. She felt a catch in her breath. "Maybe so, Hayden. It could be. Let's see how it goes after the hearings. You're political now, Hayden Bell the Fourth. This administration won't abide a Deputy Assistant Secretary living in sin."

"No. They won't." Hands on both her shoulders, his eyes deep grey, no color at all. This must be the truth, she thought. "But the hearings. People ask about domestic help, for Christ's sake. As if we could ever have afforded domestic help. The hearings—after the hearings and the nomination goes through. I'll think of you every minute. We can't let this go."

"No." She hadn't realized it. It was too precious to let go. But what was it? And she saw he meant both things. Both the position and her. "No, we'll never let it go."

"You didn't tell me your story. I told you mine."

"Saved it. I'll tell you someday. I promise."

"Good," he said. "Good girl."

The scent of him lingered from the t-shirt she wore, loose, falling over her shoulder. She gripped it, pulled it tighter around her. Change the sheets, she told herself. Get rid of the morning residue she hated after other nights, other men. She ripped off the bedding, took off the t-shirt, dumped it all in the hamper. She needed to shower, not wait for morning.

She dressed for sleep, settled into her clean bedding, relieved to be alone. Alone, she could imagine the afternoon over again, all the touches and caresses, all the sweet moments listening to the birds and hearing his lovely voice, Hank telling his sad story about boot camp and Randy Root. Now that he was away from her, she could hold him more gently in mind. Had Randy died? When she went to see Hank after the hearings, would she go to the mall, look for Randy Root on the list of names on the black wall?

Hearings. The questionnaire. She knows that one so well. They look at income tax. They want stock portfolios. They want to know what you've experimented with and with whom. They ask you what names you've used in your life. Would she be questioned? Would he put her name on the form? Would they ask her about him, the man who had been her boss, her colleague for over a decade and now, what was he? Her lover? Awkward Victorian word: lover. Her Squeeze. Her Boy. Or her *Man*, like some blues tune.

She didn't want to consider what she might be. She imagined the warm touch of him, how soothed she had felt and soon, she dreamed about their reunion getting off the plane at Dulles. He would be outside the gate ready to pull her up to him, wrap her safely up. She slipped into the quiet doze she loved so much that came before sleep or after sex or, sometimes, in that strange, in-between moment before awakening to question, for instance, who that visitor might have been, what he had done, what he had failed to do, and what he might do now.

To her. To anyone. To Randy Root, seaman recruit.

Good, he'd said to her, his last words. Good girl.

Personal Effects

The chief master-at-arms snapped off the padlock with his bolt cutters. Usually, bolt cutters show up during surprise inspections when sailors forget their own combinations owing to the contents of something embarrassing. Dope. Food. Stolen goods. Anything. But bolt cutters are also used to open lockers left behind for any reason. Sailors do that, leave their lockers behind when they transfer—sometimes full, sometimes emptied—but nonetheless, locked.

Of course, this sailor had died.

A seaman apprentice who had known the dead man was supposed to take the personal effects out of the locker and pack them in the cardboard boxes. The chief master-at-arms was supposed to list all the things in the locker on an inventory sheet, seal the boxes, and take them to the supply officer for shipping to the next of kin. The observing officer was an ensign who thought he might be there to keep track of the money. In those days, sailors were still paid in cash. Twenty-dollar bills populated ships and holed up inside sailors' lockers, and the ensign decided his job must be to ensure nothing was stolen, money or anything else for that matter. It was the ensign's second day on board and his first real task in the Navy. He was confused and hung over. He was almost twenty-three years old, had gone to a good university, had been awarded a good degree with his commission, and he was used to being sure of himself. He thought he knew what he was supposed to be doing, but he did not.

The chief stood back, let the seaman take off the remnants of the lock and lit a cigarette. In those days, we called his type a Ho Chi Minh chief, meaning he'd gotten his promotions in Vietnam for doing what they did there—meaning he had never been taught his seagoing job. These were the sorts of chief petty officers assigned to positions like chief master-at-arms since they didn't have to operate much of anything except the bolt cutter. When the seaman unhooked the hasp and the locker lid supporting the dead man's mattress popped up, the chief exhaled a billow of smoke. "Crammed-ass full. Look at that shit they keep in their lockers, now."

By then, all the old ticking mattresses were gone, and everyone had a locker the size of his rack under a foam mattress, the locker deep enough to stand a paperback book upright. Coffin lockers, we called them, stacked three high in every berthing compartment. The dead sailor had been relatively junior; his bunk had been the bottom one where those above you step past your face to climb up. The seaman sat cross-legged on the deck in the narrow aisle between the stacks of coffin lockers and racks, started to take the things out, and name them for the chief to write down. "Three pair of socks. Four skivvies. Two handkerchiefs, no three, no... six."

"Three pairs-of-socks, four-skivvies and how many-the-fuck handkerchiefs?" said the chief around his cigarette. "Just look at that shit. Huh!" He had a thin little mustache and the ensign thought he looked a lot like the actor Clark Gable except his eyes were closer together. The chief said, "Slow down, Lawton, I can't write that fast."

"Ok, Chief. Six handkerchiefs, I think. There might be some more here."

"We'll say six. Keep going. You only got an hour until the mess line closes. Look at that fucking goat rope. Didn't he ever wash his civvies? My mama always told me to wear clean skivvies in case I got in a car accident or something."

"Here's another pair of socks."

The chief master-at-arms was right, thought the ensign, No one would ever want anyone else to see this mess. Everything wrinkled, worn, crammed in, wadded together. Something smelled off. Like bad fish. It was all skewed, strange, and like everything else on this ship, very different than what he had expected, all of it different from the very first moment he'd arrived the day before, lugging his duffel, suitcase, and briefcase with his orders.

For years, the ensign had envisioned skipping up the brow of his first ship with sparkling water below, a promising sunrise and sharp sailors to greet him. Of course, he knew that such imaginings were always in error—nothing is ever the way you expect it to be. But this? This was some kind of rude joke, the ship up on blocks, trapped in one of the graving docks dug into the ground of the Brooklyn Naval Shipyard. A roaring sound had come from the ship as if some berserk engine had lost its muffler. Gouts of dust billowed out from the ship's decks, gave every surface and, now, his uniform a grimy coat.

Three grungy sailors had been on their knees doing some kind of work and blocking the ship's brow. Their breaths steamed to match the discharge oozing from outlets in the ship's hull; liquid drooled out in a slow, long fall to spatter on the dry dock floor.

But the worst of it—the petty officer had not let him on board. At the foot of the brow he had waited, his luggage piled around him, halted from going on board to report for duty while the three sailors finished reeving a web of line between the lower two cables of the lifelines. And slow? They had been dead slow, as if they were being purposefully clumsy in order to irritate the new officer. Perhaps it was some sort of hazing, a prank. But he decided they weren't being insubordinate; they were only cold and stiff, wearing their thin foul-weather jackets, their uniform watch caps, ragged gloves. The ensign himself had put on his warmest dress blues and his new pea coat with the gold buttons, a white scarf and his new gloves, as he had been told to do when reporting aboard. Even so, he had been naked cold in the small breeze mumbling from a dirty sky.

When the roaring had finally stopped for a breath, a petty officer in his dress blues had called down from the ship's deck. "It'll be just a second, sir. Ops says nobody steps foot on the brow until we get the man-saver rigged."

"Who?"

"The operations officer, sir, he closed the brow."

Could the brow have actually been closed off to him? After all, he was an *officer*. The petty officer's haircut was way out of regulation; it fluttered too long onto the collar of his pea coat. His shoes looked like they had never been shined. He wore a filthy, yellow hardhat instead of the bright, white sailor's dixie cup the ensign had expected.

Then the roar had returned full on wild and hollow, trembling in his chest. Anything to escape it. And the cold. His Corfam shoes—so convenient at school for their permanent shine—absolutely no fucking good. He thought of simply bulling his way aboard. That might look bad, though, his first day. The ensign cupped his hands around his mouth and hollered back to the petty officer, "Very well," as they had taught him to say.

In three years and ten months, the ensign would detach from the ship. He would be a lieutenant, and confident. With his new rank on his collar, he would stroll down the brow half-saddened, half-elated with his tour of duty after hundreds of hours in the pilothouse charged with the ship's movement and safety, proud of his authority and competence, happy for the way his body had learned the dip and roll of an agile vessel at sea. He would be older and stronger, wiser and better. In sixteen years he would have command of a destroyer, then a cruiser. He would be powerful and good.

But none of that was conceivable to him when the petty officer finally waved him aboard. He saluted the ship's fantail as he had been taught and yelled over the roar, "Reporting aboard for duty!" Even though what he wanted to say was, is this the right place? Isn't there another frigate with the same name somewhere else, taut and clean? Isn't there some other ship that looks bigger, brighter, newer? Isn't there some mistake?

As the ensign watched Seaman Apprentice Lawton unpack the dead man's locker, he couldn't help but think how different the boy looked from the dirty petty officer on the quarterdeck and how much the same. Lawton was neat, well groomed, his dungarees kept clean despite all the dust from the grinding. But he had the same sort of reticence as the petty officer, a kind of distance or reserve. The seaman removed a leather holster from the locker, took out an oversized pocket knife. The sheath looked like something a sailor would make for himself out of boredom and pride. The seaman stared at the knife for a moment, turned it gingerly over, and the ensign thought the seaman wanted to ask if he could keep it. But he set it carefully onto his lap, leaned forward over it, stuck his palms up into his eye sockets. His shoulders started to quiver. He looked like he was trying not to cry. He *was* crying.

"Lawton," said the chief master-at-arms. "Hey. Seaman Lawton. Whyn't you go on up topside and take a smoke break, ok?"

"I'm ok, Chief." The seaman wiped the sleeve of his dungaree shirt under his nose.

"Just go on and do what I told you." The chief narrowed his eyes at the ensign, gestured toward the seaman with his cigarette.

"Yes," said the ensign, awakened that he could do something. "Yes. It will be fine, Seaman Lawton. You go ahead. We'll take care of this."

"Thank you, sir. I'll be all right in a minute, sir. I'm sorry."

And the ensign said, "Don't worry, Seaman. I understand."

The chief master-at-arms stood motionless, his khaki uniform faded shades lighter than issue, but starched into submission. The ensign had expected him to say something about Lawton when the seaman was up the ladder out of earshot, but he pointed to the locker with his cigarette. "Sir. Uh. Would you mind taking the things out of the locker? I already started the inventory." He glanced at the clipboard in his hands.

The ensign felt that perhaps he and the chief shared some sort of kinship. He decided that the chief's nod and narrowed eyes must be some sort of secret sign between them to look out for a sailor who was obviously mourning. And while he knew that officers weren't supposed to do this sort of work, unpack a locker, he decided that it would be the best choice for him to pick up the slack for Lawton under the circumstances. He decided that a confident officer would answer as he did. "No. I don't mind at all, Chief. No sweat."

These lockers usually get a smell that is like a distillation of the berthing compartment itself. Deodorant, tobacco, soap, shaving cream, aftershave we called foo-foo juice inevitably spilled inside the locker and never cleaned up. Not unpleasant. But this one smelled sweaty and old. Grimy civilian jeans. Wadded up t-shirts. Unwashed socks. An open and dried Old Spice stick moldered in a corner, the only reasonable odor.

"Look at this, Chief." Surprised, and now a little put out that he had to handle all this squalid clothing, the ensign held up a dungaree shirt. "Look at this. I thought this guy's name was White." The shirt had been stenciled 'Johanson.'

"Thief," said the chief master-at-arms. He picked a bit of tobacco lint off his tongue. "I figure White for a thief. Whole division is a bunch of thieves."

"What do we do?"

"Johanson got out. So it'll go in the lucky bag for the numbskull who spends all his money and loses his uniforms. We don't ship that sort of shit home to surprise grandma."

The ensign considered that statement for a moment and decided to treat it as good advice from a Trusted Advisor.

Obviously this chief knew what he was doing. He decided his trust was warranted as they found other things they didn't pack up. The half-empty toothpaste tubes. A pile of *Hustler* magazines with pages folded back to reveal open, greasy vaginas. A collection of small stones. Something from some beach somewhere.

"Just dirt," the chief master-at-arms declared looking at the two condoms the ensign set aside without asking. "Fat, fucking chance he ever got to use them things. Wishful fucking thinking. But hoooly shit lookee here!"

The ensign didn't see anything. "What?"

"Don't you see that there, sir? That there's ship's equipment. None of that there shit is supposed to be anywhere but in the workspaces, sir. Here, lemme..." The chief master-at-arms reached down into the locker, picked up a crescent wrench and two screwdrivers. He pointed at an issue flashlight. "We need to write that up, sir."

He held up the tools in front of the ensign's face, too close.

"Put a dead sailor on report?" The ensign stared up at him.

"Look. sir. Of course you can't put a dead sailor on report. But this here berthing compartment? We need to get down here and figure out what's up. Fucking thieves. You seen it. You know how many goddam tools we lose a year, sir? Lots." He shook the wrench and screwdrivers as if he was about to club something.

"What, we're supposed to stop right now, start inspecting lockers?"

"Well, they're going to be your division, sir. You can't let them get away with thinking you're some kind of pushover. You got to assert yourself, sir. Or that's what they'll think you are, a pushover."

The ensign decided there wasn't any kinship with this chief. He had been wrong. This was all some sort of hazing or bullying or something. Like seeing who could eat an onion the fastest, or chug a full quart of beer, or the shaving cream he'd been forced to inject into the top of his trousers for his fraternity. A test or indoctrination or whatever you called it; all of it was the same thing—someone forced you to do something ridiculous and you did it, knowing it was ridiculous, but did it anyway. He might only be twenty-two years old, but he could recognize the source of this kind of treatment, something to laugh about in the chiefs' mess. The ensign didn't have to pay any attention to this sort of thing. Not at all. Anymore.

"We'll finish the inventory, Chief. I'll talk to my department head."

"You don't know how quick these lockers will empty out, sir. Everything in the trash. We need to seal the compartment and do a locker check this afternoon."

"Later, Chief."

"Aye, sir," he oozed with his best chief's voice. Then, like all the bullies the ensign had ever known, he couldn't keep himself from trying to make the victim think it was his own fault. "I'll talk to the executive officer about it."

What would the XO do? Would he do anything? Would the chief even say anything to the ship's second-in-command? Not even a real bully. A chicken-shit tattletale. Christ, it was like third grade. Well. If the ensign was doing wrong, it was out of a good sense, the kind of good sense he'd always been told he possessed. And there was that old Navy saying, something like: it's better to beg forgiveness later than ask for permission now.

The ensign had been told how to end conversations like this. "Very well, Chief." The man grew silent, as all bullies do when they don't get their own way.

They inventoried twenty-six dollars and fourteen cents. Counted twice, the money was sealed in a separate envelope, a fat collection of dimes, nickels, and dollar bills picked out of the bottom of the locker. The ensign thought they were done. And maybe the chief master-at-arms was right. Maybe they needed to search the other lockers in the compartment. But it was a dumb idea—seal off the berthing compartment right now. It was almost lunchtime, and everyone would want to get back down in the compartment. Besides, he was ready for lunch himself. A chance to spend some more time with other junior officers around the dinner table in the wardroom, those other officers who had turned out to be such good company last night. His head still felt as thick as wet felt, but it had been a great welcome.

On the quarterdeck the day before, nobody would have ever convinced him that anything was going to turn out even halfway decent. The dirty petty officer had been nice enough; he'd even given him two little pieces of yellow foam, "Ear protection!" he'd hollered and then showed him how to cram them into his ears. But they seemed to have no effect against that unbelievable howl.

"*Yard birds!*" the petty officer had yelled at him and pointed forward on the main deck. Three people—men or women, he couldn't be sure in their filthy, homeless-person rags— wrestled the handles of roaring steel machines billowing out dirt and debris.

"*Shipyard workers taking up the decks.*" The ensign realized they were grinding up the ship's weather decks, using mechanical crawlers to hammer the old epoxy-based paint off the steel.

"They been working on it for a week." The petty officer looked as stricken as if he'd been the victim of an accident. "Here, sit inside the deckhouse until somebody comes to get you, sir. It won't be so noisy."

It hadn't made any difference. It seemed as though the ensign had to wait forever while the petty officer phoned different places looking for someone who was supposed to be welcoming him. Finally, an officer had shown up, the communications officer, and the ensign had been very relieved that finally he would be able to get inside the ship to get away. No one had told him it would be worse inside. A scum of grit on every railing, chair and desk. And the noise? It had felt as though he were inside a steel drum while madmen with clubs beat the top. He'd had to endure that amplified roar the whole time he was checked in, issued a hardhat to protect his head from those things that fell during yard periods, fitted for other earplugs that worked only a little better. He spent ten minutes meeting the ship's wiry little XO who was too busy to holler anything more than "Welcome aboard!" and tell him that the captain would be back off leave next week.

He was given a stateroom and told he would share it with another ensign. It had a fold-out desk and a small personal safe. He was given a combination and told to keep his valuables in the safe or the yard birds would rip him off. There was no mattress on the bed. All of the officers' mattresses were off the ship to keep them from being ruined by the dirt. He was told only the duty officers slept on board, all this before he'd even gotten out of his dress uniform.

Finally, the communications officer had helped him drag his baggage off the ship to a row of abandoned brownstones peering high over the shipyard, built for long-gone senior staff, their families and retainers. In the only brownstone without plywood over the windows, the frigate's officers had rigged their mattresses on cots in the empty rooms and gotten the shipyard to turn on the heat, so they could use the building when they were in the off-duty section. There were hot showers, bare walls of peeled paint, no furniture, no curtains.

That's when he found out about the dead man. The communications officer told him that the dead man had come back to the ship drunk after a night in Manhattan. He had started up the brow and the watch had thought he was doing fine. But they had looked away, and he'd disappeared. Slipped under the lifelines. He'd dropped to the dry dock floor. The tired, dirty petty officer had witnessed the sailor's last living movement, the insentient stretching of his limbs like a bug crushed underfoot.

The communications officer was the one who told the ensign that tomorrow it would be his job to inventory the dead man's personal effects. Had he lived, the dead sailor would have been one of the ensign's subordinates, part of the Communications Division. The communications officer would have been doing the inventory himself, but he had to fly home with the body.

The ensign was given a room on the third story of the townhouse, bare, two cots, one set up and swaddled in bedding and beat-up pillows, the other folded. There were no closets, no sets of drawers or lockers. Some roommate had already taken the side of the room farthest from the door and stacked his clothing in piles against the wall. The communications officer told him to unpack, then get into his working uniform, hurry back to the ship.

The ensign had taken his uniforms out of their bags, his civilian clothing, toiletries and underwear, lined all of it up along a mildewed wall in a forlorn heap with the grey air rattling through the dry window sash, the bare bulb glaring overhead. He changed into his newest khakis that would now be ruined by all the dirt. He wandered his way back to the ship past great, rusted architectures of abandoned cranes, steel plates, past the sulfurous spew of arc welders spattering the ground and toward the noise still battling its way into the air from those grinders. He blundered through the rest of the day, found himself introduced to the other officers at dinner, the grinders finally quiet. There was some pleasantry, handshakes and welcomes aboard. Then there was nothing to do. Not even a functioning TV in the wardroom.

It had been dark when he tried to walk back to the brownstone. He got turned around, finally found it, and made his way up to the room with the single light bulb. He had never felt more alone in his entire life.

He hadn't even taken off his shoes when the communications officer banged on his door and rustled him up to participate in what he was told had become a local custom, unique to his frigate and only observed for this one season in this particular shipyard.

Even years later, as an old man, he would look at the photo taken that night with genuine happiness. There, in the massive living room of the old brownstone, holding up what may have been his fourth or tenth bottle of Rolling Rock, flanked on either side by the operations officer, the communications officer, and as many other officers as would fit, also holding up their beers, all of them in full, drunken roar to Springsteen's "Born to Run," all of them perched high up on the massive mantel of that Civil War-era fireplace in their jeans and t-shirts, ragged short haircuts, birth control eyeglasses and in their homesickness for their families in Norfolk, forever performing what they would all recall as a Mantel Dance.

The ensign dropped the top of the dead man's locker with a slam, stood and stretched. That Mantle Dance had been the sort of kinship he thought he could trust. Those officers were his shipmates, not this chief master-at-arms. Seal off the berthing compartment, no way. Now all he wanted to do is get back up to the wardroom for lunch where he could bitch with everyone else about his hangover, eat. And the chief master-at-arms was another prick fucking with him just for fun. So much for this. "Good work, Chief. We'll do something about those tools later."

"Uh, sir." The chief master-at-arms nodded at the bank of small gym lockers. "We need to do the upright locker, too."

Of course, there would be another locker. They could do it after lunch. But the chief was too quick, the lock clipped away before he could say anything.

There they were: four fat stacks, neater than anything else in either locker, letters bound up with rubber bands and saved for some future the dead sailor had imagined.

Nothing to be done with it now, and there didn't seem to be that much else other than those letters. The ensign took the first packet down, "One stack of letters." He knelt down to place them in the box with the clothing, waited for the chief master-at-arms to write it down.

There are no more Ho Chi Minh Chiefs. And these days, the ship's chief master-at-arms is a different animal. Today, that job has its own rating; people train for it. Back then, nobody wanted to be the ship's cop. But what else could the chief do? What did he know about ships after three tours in Vietnam? He was one hundred ninety-three days and a wake-up from transfer ashore; he did the best he felt like doing on any particular day, at any particular moment. He knew a lot about dead men, and he told the ensign, "Sir. You've got to keep the letters aside."

The ensign didn't say anything. On his knees in front of the locker, he looked up to hear the chief master-at-arms say, "You have to read them, sir."

The packet was almost too fat for the ensign to grip with one hand. At least a hundred letters. More. And three other packets. Four hundred letters. Classic. It would take him forever. Everything took forever. There it was again, the sense that none of this was real, all of it some sort of joke.

A skipping sound like a hammer's tap started above him, then it bit down on the steel, the stunning malice of a mechanical grinder directly over his head.

All along, the ensign had thought perhaps that this whole assignment to inventory the locker had been another rite of passage: get the ensign drunk at the Mantel Dance, give him a hangover, make him stay under the grinders with the special attraction of getting to know the chief master-at-arms who let his cigarette ashes drop onto the deck, the smoke peeling up into the berthing compartment as the ensign looked at four fat packages of letters.

"Read them, sir. You've got to read them letters."

"I *heard* you, Chief."

Oh bullshit, the ensign thought. He was going to fall for this? Read them? Bullshit. None of this was feeling right. As far as he was concerned, this whole thing seemed staged for the chief master-at-arms to get someone else to do his job. *He should be taking things out and the ensign should be writing the inventory. This bit about reading the letters? Bullshit.* He was about to tell him exactly that, "Bullshit," when the chief master-at-arms billowed smoke all over and yelled above the noise, "*Regulation! And I can't watch you. You got to do it alone. Never know what people will put in a letter, sir!*"

Another sound. Some sort of chatter, louder. Another sort of hammer to bang the paint off the ship's decks. The chief master-at-arms said something else.

The ensign couldn't understand over the noise. "*WHAT?*"

He cupped his hands around his mouth, bellowed, "*Stateroom! STATEROOM. Take them to your stateroom, you don't have to read them here.*"

The ensign looked at the bundles. Oh God, it would take hours. Why read them? Of course, he decided, maybe there was something in these letters the family shouldn't see, like those bare women in those magazines. But.

"Two." He held up two fingers. "*Two for the inventory? Don't we both have to do it?*" He pointed quickly at the chief, then at himself.

The chief master-at-arms leaned down, cupped his hands around the ensign's ear. He smelled exactly like the berthing compartment—coffee, cigarettes, and aftershave. "Look, sir. Who knows what you'll find with these assholes? And White was no princess. You're an *officer*, sir. If you say the letters are all in the box, they are *all* in the box. I got *faith* in you, ensign."

After he finally left the chief master-at-arms, after his headache faded and the day drew to an end, and after the grinding mercifully stopped, the ensign found the wardroom for his dinner. It was nearly empty, only three other officers. It was the Friday of the President's Day holiday in February, a three-day weekend. The officers had arranged to leave only a few on board to keep watch while all the others either drove back to Norfolk to see their families or got out in the town for some fun. As he had expected, the junior guy, George, would most certainly be one of the luckless four left on board until Tuesday morning. And they were truly stuck; the duty officers couldn't even leave the ship to sleep in the brownstone, but had to stay in case of fire or other emergency. He sat down to eat with Ops and two other junior officers thinking he was going to tell them about that asshole chief master-at-arms. But the more senior officers had other ideas.

Ops would detach in a year to disappear from the ensign's life forever. One of the junior officers would be accepted for flight school, fly jets, then go on to become a lawyer. The other, the ship's disbursing officer, would become the ensign's friend for life. But all of them were strangers to him at dinner that first duty night, staring, smiling, nodding to each other as if they were wary grifters about to take his money when Ops looked up from his plate of tepid chili-mac and green beans, leveled his coke bottle glasses at the ensign, and said, "Play bridge?"

For an instant, the ensign thought he was talking about the Brooklyn Bridge. Then he realized he meant the card game. The ensign did not play bridge.

"Then, we think it's time you learned."

That weekend, they set their own routine. The shipyard knocked off work for all three days; the grinding stopped. When the steam supply from the shipyard began to weaken and when the heating began to go, they fixed it themselves. The ensign watched as two of the crew used the chief master-at-arms' bolt cutters to relieve a lock from the cage on a steam valve, hooked up a hose to supply the ship, and cracked the valve open to feed the ship's galley and living areas. "Don't ever tell anyone you saw them do that," Ops told him.

The two other junior officers took the ensign with them when they went on watch to huddle in a quarterdeck shack at the top of the brow in emulation of the dirty petty officer. Four hours at a shot, twice a day, he crouched over an electric space heater and listened while they taught him what he needed to know to be an officer of the deck in port. They slept pretty much when they wanted to sleep, ate the meals when they were readied three times a day, and played, in between, thirty-one rubbers of contract bridge.

The ensign had never before liked playing card games, but they all agreed he had a natural sense. And for the ensign, the whole idea of bidding, setting the contract, the silent complicity with a partner to break your opponent, win a hand or a game, that give and take across the table seemed so natural and comfortable—by Sunday he was dreaming about bridge, by Monday he was imagining hands every waking moment, those brilliant auctions when he and his partner would arrive at a suit and number only to see the play fall out exactly as envisioned.

He had never felt less alone.

Forever after that long weekend, he would find himself sought out by the more skilled players as the preferred "newbie" partner, as they would seek him out to stand watch with them. He would be known as a particularly diligent and competent junior officer.

Perhaps because he felt so comfortable about learning bridge, perhaps the grey cold of Brooklyn, the oily dirt of the shipyard, the newness of everything, his own confusion, perhaps the decisions he'd made. He would never know what it was, perhaps sloth. He never read the letters.

When the crew and the officers returned from the holiday, he sealed up the boxes with Seaman Lawton who seemed fine, relieved even to be shipping his friend's effects away to the designated next of kin. The chief master-at-arms had signed the inventories without even looking at them, and the ensign had placed a copy of the inventory inside each box, and kept a copy for himself as someone had told him to do. He gave a copy to the ship's admin officer for the ship's records. That copy stayed in a file cabinet until IT advances let the ship go paperless and the inventory found itself shredded with all those other old records no one has ever used or wanted.

The inventory did not mention letters. As he put them into his small safe, spun the combination closed, the ensign told himself he would forward the letters to the next of kin later. In the safe, they left barely enough room for his wallet. They smelled like the dead man's coffin locker along with talcum or shaving cream, a stack of multicolored paper: white, grayed plain envelopes, some pastels and yellows, different sizes.

When the cold weather lifted and days grew longer and warm, they took in the brow, filled the dry dock and refloated without incident. A wheezing old tug towed them to a pier where they started coaxing the boilers to life. There, after they cleaned away all the filth of the grinding, welding and ordinary neglect, the ensign moved the letters into the small safe of his permanent stateroom.

By the first day of summer, the ship had emerged from the shipyard, turned smartly out of the shipyard estuary into Wallabout Bay and—snapping with signal flags, pennants, the ship's battle ensign rippling from the masthead—they stood down the channel transformed into the fine vessel the ensign had always imagined. He took his first watch in the pilothouse that sea detail while the operations officer and the captain threaded the ship out of the Hudson River, past the estuary and beyond all sight of land. There, a brilliant ocean breeze and swell answered all the ensign's dreams of going to sea, and the frigate began its normal daily routine, cast off from any real memory of graving docks.

He didn't have much to do with the chief master-at-arms after the inventory. When they saw each other, he would nod, "Chief," to hear the response, "Ensign," and he decided this was a sign of respect he'd earned and now shared, a professional consideration from an experienced older man to a younger, but more senior man who had done the right thing. The chief master-at-arms transferred into retirement and that reminder too was gone.

After the ensign became a lieutenant, after he learned all the small and large skills he would need to conn a ship, he strolled down the brow half-saddened, half-elated with his tour of duty, proud of his authority and competence, happy for the way his body knew the dip and roll of an agile vessel at sea, and relieved to be finished with his first ship and off to the life he had decided. He was older and stronger, wiser and better. He took his safe combination with him.

The new ensign who was assigned his old stateroom was unable to open the safe; nobody could find the combination. The new ensign asked around and was told he needed to submit something called a two-kilo to have the shipyard's locksmith come over to fix it. That ensign locked his cash and other valuables in a desk drawer with a hasp and a padlock and actually submitted a two-kilo late in his tour when someone showed him how to do so. But by the time the shipyard responded, he'd been transferred; nobody knew what the locksmith was supposed to do when he showed up to fix some lock somewhere on board. The new officer in the stateroom didn't know anything about any locksmith and understood that the safe was broken and couldn't be fixed.

Someday, someone would open the safe and find the letters. They would smell like talcum, shampoo and dust. They would tell no story. They would be thoughts from a father, a mother, a brother, and friends shared with a boy they missed. There would be best wishes for Christmas and a birthday or two, descriptions of Easter and Thanksgiving dinners, news of the new mall, the widened highway, a grandfather's illness and recovery.

Perhaps they would be sent, finally returned to those who wrote them. Or perhaps the officer who found them would think it was too late to send them, their very lateness calling into question the integrity, the fairness, and the goodness of his service and the Navy. Perhaps the officer will read them, as they had once been read, and cherish their simple affection as much as the dead sailor had been cherished by those who wrote those letters about their everyday lives.

But I don't know this. This is only speculation and not at all part of this story.

THE MOUSE

MORNING WATCH

ZERO THREE THIRTY—0330—has always been the normal hour to relieve the morning watch, the watch associated with the rise of spirits brought on by the smell of night-baking newly out of a ship's ovens and the dawn over the sea. Of course, in the Pentagon, there is no night-baking. Nor is there a true dawn, only the maze of corridors and offices, empty and the same, where at 0330 one Saturday morning, Commander James Ehrlich found himself stabbing his key code onto the tiny buttons of an electronic lock. When it failed to click open, he was first irritated, then puzzled, then resigned to find himself in front of the wrong door on the wrong floor without actually remembering his half-asleep stumble up from the vast east parking lot, up all those echoing stairs.

He corrected himself. He turned, made his way up another flight. At least he'd made it to the right section, the outermost of the building's concentric rings, the E-ring, where his boss, the admiral, could look out of his office to see Arlington National Cemetery, and in those days, the gravestones had not yet crept down onto the flat, treeless lawns but remained still within the deep shade of the mature trees planted for wars long past.

Ehrlich's desk had no view of Arlington. His cubicle was housed in the inner side of the ring with a view into the bleak stone of air corridors built to cool the building in the 1940s. The windows had long been sealed shut and gave the inner offices no fresh air, only an ill, indirect light. He could see nothing now, of course. Dark. He flipped on the lights.

Mildew

What was he doing rising out of his warm bed to trundle into his office on a Saturday? He had been recently promoted to the rank of commander; at sea, he would have been considered too senior for this sort of assignment. But by Pentagon standards, he was only senior enough to be considered trustworthy. No one thought twice about giving him this early morning task, and he was presumed to still have the energy and optimism required to go in to work at what he thought of as Zero Three Dead-Fucking-Dark Thirty on a Saturday morning to write a point paper for the admiral to read at 8 AM sharp.

If asked, he would have said he felt only a little disappointment about the early hour. His wife and their toddler were living in Norfolk, but he still might make it home for half of Saturday and all of Sunday. And it could have been worse. His most recent ship was at sea. Had he been aboard, there would have been no chance to spend any of the weekend at home. A half-weekend with his wife and son was a vast improvement, and he was telling himself that he could write the book of Genesis from scratch and still hit the road for home by noon when he saw the small, gray, Pentagon mouse. On his desk. Rigidly adhered to the sticky paper of the modern mousetrap someone had set yesterday evening after Ehrlich had left work for beers and sea stories with the other geographic bachelors.

He shifted in his seat. The mouse followed him with its eye. Not an accusation. Not even fear, a single moving eye, dark, unblinking and dying.

Ehrlich noted the scent of mildew. But this was nothing new. He had been back in the Pentagon long enough to have reduced this mildew odor to a subliminal nod, part of the atmosphere but not important—unlike the day of his arrival when, out of habit, the scent had been of concern to him. Had he smelt anything like this on his ship, he would have had sailors on their knees scrubbing the starch out of the space and ventilating it, airing it, returning the area to the level of tolerance one requires to survive in any meaningful fashion at sea. Ashore, there were other standards, and it was axiomatic that a month on station wiped out any standard from the previous duty station, where, in Ehrlich's case, he had set the standard as the executive officer of USS Ferrell, the ship off the Virginia coast, keeping its families from home that very morning.

Old XO—XO—New XO

In fact, at that moment, the morning watch on Ferrell was in the process of relieving the midwatch, and the officers and sailors were as cranky as two-year-olds about staying at sea over the weekend to do casualty control drills on the engineering plant. Ehrlich had not been away long enough for the ship's memory of him to fade; he was still referred to as the Old XO. They had a New XO who seemed a lot like the Old XO to the crew and as a result, Ehrlich would soon be forgotten, and no one would refer to him at all on *USS Ferrell*. Some papers he had signed would remain for a while, but they, too, would soon be gone and those who had served with him would soon forget his given name. He would be remembered as the old XO, the new XO, my XO or sometimes even, our XO.

In the Pentagon, Ehrlich had become OPNAV N524a. No one reported to him, he was responsible for no one but himself. Four officers more senior to him were his bosses, but no one even referred to him unless it was to ask for a point paper first thing on Saturday morning. They certainly didn't expect him to worry about mildew as he had when he'd been XO. In the Pentagon, as OPNAV N524a, mildew was no longer his watch.

LUCKY

As for mildew, Ehrlich was particularly sensitive to the scent that morning on account of the mouse stuck to his desk. "Mold means mice, mice mean mold," is what his mother used to say when he was a boy and it was his mother's admonition he heard rather than the other possible thought, his memory of Lucky, the mouse he'd owned as a ten-year-old and for whom, despite all threats from his parents, he had found a mate through purchase at the pet store where they were kept to feed snakes. The mate and Lucky had enthusiastically produced a mouse explosion, heavily inbred and quickly diseased until his father found this secret stash, a mouse holocaust, all the animals starved into cannibalism because the boyhood version of Ehrlich had lost interest in them.

His father brought the whole deformed, ravenous cage of Lucky's offspring back to the delighted pet store owners with their snakes.

Ehrlich never lost interest again.

This probably formed the basis for the splendid concern he developed for his subordinates, a reputation for diligence that had made him a good XO and earned him a life writing point papers in the Pentagon.

HUMAN REMAINS

What was the purpose of this point paper? Some task of extreme national importance? Not really. It is sufficient to say that it would cause six people to work at some time over their weekend. By Tuesday, the point paper Ehrlich was to write and revise eight times would find itself overtaken by events and abandoned in a file folder for the next thirteen years until Flight 77 would cauterize it along with the mildew and the mice who infested that section of the building.

Flight 77 will not cauterize Ehrlich. By then he will have long been promoted to captain and will have commenced his graceful slide toward retirement. He will find himself at the US Embassy in Rome as the planes hit, wondering *what-the-fuck?* as three of his friends along with a couple thousand other people in the Pentagon, Manhattan and Pennsylvania shared their versions of *what-the-fuck?* before finding themselves reduced to human remains.

AFFECTION

One of these friends was on the USS Ferrell that very morning, awake and standing watch. At the moment Ehrlich and the mouse gazed at each other, this friend, a shipmate of sorts, happily imagined Ehrlich, his old XO, asleep at home with his family.

This is the affection of shipmates.

It, the ship—especially a destroyer like their ship—can create a special bond between people. Ehrlich had been his shipmate's immediate superior. The shipmate had been the operations officer, or Ops.

These names, XO, Ops, Captain, are immutable. Years after the fact they will be remembered, and in certain circumstances former shipmates refer to each other by the names they used when they knew each other best. When Ehrlich finally gets a phone to work in Rome, when he finally speaks with someone who knows what's going on at the burning Pentagon, it will be his former captain he reaches. Nearly a decade and a half will have gone by since his time on Ferrell and the morning he found the dying mouse, but he will still feel like that man's XO when he hears his former captain say, "Did you know Ops was in the building? Did you know he was in his office?"

At that instant, he will become the XO again. This man will be his captain again, and the blame for his shipmate's death will feel as though it was somehow his blame. Even though he will always know that nothing could have been done, he will hope that Ops had been content. He will hope that Ops had been at peace with himself.

Ops

In fact, on 9/11, Ops will be feeling specifically grateful and relieved by the little break from sea duty until the news of the burning twin towers popped up on CNN. He had been looking forward to a few years away from standing watch, the narrow staterooms, the sheer release from the responsibility for another three hundred souls. He'll think it's good to get a little breather before he goes back to sea. But as he bends over his computer screen to plan contingencies for immediate response to the initial attack on New York, (not having any answers but working nonetheless) he will look up at the television to see the second aircraft plow into the tower, and at that moment, he will wish he was at sea.

There was something that draws them to ships.

Especially in these moments when they think of all the possible things that might have been done to prevent those aircraft from their obscene turn into those buildings, all the moments that could have been seized to prevent that astonishing revelation of failure—especially in those moments—it is the ship itself that draws them, their familiar place, their practiced home where they had been shipmates together.

There is no such thing as a shipmate in the Pentagon.

On the day of the attack, there will be nothing for Ops to do. His job on the staff will have no bearing on any operation connected with defense of the homeland, nor will anyone give his section any real tasking out of the panic of that 9/11 moment in Manhattan. Like all of his colleagues, he will think that this lack of tasking is the reason he feels the pull of his ship so strongly, his recall of the notion of shipmates, their trust for each other on watch. The man who was Ops and who would soon be dust, dreams of all the moments he could have done something, *anything* better and different, all those moments when he could have cared better for shipmates. Then Flight 77 makes its incomprehensible turn, straightens, lowers, and for a while, all the mildew and mice disappear.

Rat Guards

Flight 77 was still years in the future and as unforeseeable to Ehrlich as it was to the mouse affixed to his desktop. He'd never seen this sort of mousetrap before. The method was obviously suffocation, every attempt to escape as tightening as a lie. He wondered if such a trap would work as well on a rat. Certainly they could be caught. Like mice, they will bump from one barrier to the next, instinctively searching for something to eat or some other rat with whom to mate.

But would it kill them?

Ehrlich, like every sailor, loathed rats for their internal circuitry that compelled them to seek out mooring lines. Rats breed themselves to think that those thick hawsers draped up from the pier lead to the shipload of food that oozed such an irresistible odor, the scent begged them to chase each other up from the pier, heedless of any danger or trap, and they will board, these rats, unless they are hindered by rat guards—big, round, flayed out collars of galvanized tin placed in preventive cones around every line leading up to a ship, electrical cables, phone cables and of course, the mooring lines. He'd seen wharf rats mob a ship's rat guard. Heaped atop each other, they had fallen off the lines and into the water like panicked refugees at a closed border, they lusted so. And he had imagined exactly this scenario after they had moored in Naples, a port where rats overran everything like a bad conscience.

KITA

That morning in Naples, they had tied the ship to the pier as usual, but somehow, the rat guards had not been deployed. Ehrlich had seen Ferrell's naked lines beckoning, and had imagined voracious, foreign rats already gathering to stream up in clumps. Or even two rats slipping in unnoticed. Two alone would be enough to breed across their own generations producing deformed rodents in evil droves. And they would be unhindered. The ship's sailors might have forgotten to crawl out on the mooring lines to set the rat guards, but Ehrlich had thought it more likely that someone had decided to let the duty section set up the rat guards, so the off-duty watches could get a head start on liberty ashore.

Unsat.

At that moment, as USS Ferrell's XO, Ehrlich was wholly in charge; the captain had left the ship on arrival to meet with the commodore for glasses of Prosecco, tasty pu-pus and the one-on-one visibility the captain needed to nurture his promotion. As such, Ehrlich was free to use whatever means he desired to correct the situation and forestall the inevitable rat assault. He'd been thinking lately that the ship needed a little shake-up, so he chose rage.

Rage has always been a tool in the kitbag of leadership arts. It has had its advantages and disadvantages, its adherents and detractors. There was even a formal school of management in the Navy, mutated to define rage as an acceptable and effective approach. Kick In The Ass, or KITA as it was called—such a satisfying Japanese ring to it. More thoughtful practitioners defended KITA as an essential performance skill required of every true authority figure. It was cited, sometimes, as a useful tool in battle. Others condemned it as last resort of the small-minded, the unprofessional, the defeated.

Whatever one's position on this issue, it was generally agreed that rage generates an immediate response, etches a lasting impression, and introduces the probability of future rages in the minds of a ship's crew. And rage was especially effective, as in the case of Ehrlich, when it rose out of someone who had never before let slip the sort of performance he would unleash that afternoon.

He gave some thought to his rage, then stepped out to assault the evil empire of the ship who had been so sloppy as to leave its lines ashore unprotected.

Checklist

The Naples smog cloyed the ship's quarterdeck at the head of the brow where the in-port officer of the deck, an inconsequential ensign, was already in position to manage the ship's business while tied up to a pier. There, Ehrlich found Ops as he had expected, stationed as the ship's command duty officer, the CDO, the officer who would be left in charge if Ehrlich could ever get off the ship.

If Ehrlich had known that Ops was destined for Flight 77, he might have chosen a less rage-like response. But of course, no one can foresee which errors they will truly regret and which will be forgotten. As it was, his consideration, instinct, experience and crankiness from short sleep and long hours at sea demanded that he apply the same sort of punishing, unanswerable questions others had flame-sprayed onto his skin when he'd been an ensign as inconsequential as the officer of the deck who hid behind the CDO. He chose to start with, "Officer of the Deck, do you notice anything wrong as you look down along the pier?"

Ops shuttled sideways into Ehrlich's line of sight. He didn't want to stick up for the ensign. But he knew he was expected to intervene.

Ops said, "No, sir," before the ensign could immolate

himself by answering the question. This redirected Ehrlich to say:

"Ever think of using the checklist, Ops?"

AYE-AYE

The sense of relief the inconsequential ensign felt over Ops' intervention would be exquisitely remembered the day he would see Ops' name carved onto the stubby black rock they erected in Arlington to memorialize those not found after Flight 77. As he looked at the name on that stone two decades in the future, he would remember how Ops looked at the checklist, how it had the words "Install rat guards" at item number four after "Double up lines" and "Secure engines," and "Put over the gangway," and long before it said, "Request permission from the XO to pass Liberty Call."

This had been the moment when three sailors, out of uniform and readied in their liberty clothes of t-shirts, jeans and beaten jackets, wandered down to the quarterdeck in anticipation of what they had believed to be their imminent release to go ashore.

"Rat guards," said Ops. "We need to rig the rat guards."

"Rat-FUCKING-guards," Ehrlich's voice rose into a squall. "Get 'em out there! OUT! OUT!"

"Aye-aye, sir," snapped Ops. The phrase 'aye-aye' may seem a naval cliché, almost playacting, but 'aye-aye' remains in use with its strict meaning—I have heard and I will comply— along with a more complex and accurate sense: I'm junior to you. I will do what you tell me. And I hope you have said the last word to me about it because I don't want to get my ass chewed anymore.

The Rat

At this moment, a small Naples-bred rat looked up from the pier, one paw on the mooring line. His lean snout parsed the air for competent predators and the galley. He scented no danger, only some rich cooking, and still very young, not yet culled out from the more risk-averse pack, the rat stepped up and scuttled as they do in their clumsy-quick rodent way directly for USS *Ferrell's* quarterdeck.

They all saw it. The entire watch: Ops, the inconsequential ensign, the junior sailor who was the messenger of the watch, the experienced petty officer of the watch carrying a baton and a sidearm and the three sailors hoping to get ashore first. And Ehrlich, *Ferrell's* XO—all of them watched that rat clamber up the bone-white mooring line.

Rage was no longer silly playacting. Here came the first one of rats in droves waiting to board with all their twisted rat children and deformed rat spouses. Ehrlich shot his finger at the open oval in the fat steel chock where the mooring lines tumbled onto the ship to grip the double stump of the bits. He commanded: "Petty Officer of the Watch, *stand here*. Don't let that fucking rat get aboard."

Battle

Three years after leaving the Pentagon and after his encounter with the stuck mouse on his desk had long left his memory, Ehrlich would distinguish himself in battle during the first Gulf War. In command and in action, he would be calm, focused, lethal. He would engage with alacrity and precision and while his citation would not note this, he would withhold fire to accept surrender from a tiny group of terrified Iraqi sailors rather than shell them to death. He would consider that his finest moment.

However, on the quarterdeck, facing that rat, Ehrlich was not yet the naval officer he would become. He raged to Ops, "*Get the fucking rat guards out, out, out!!*" He snatched up the microphone of the ship's general announcing system and raged for the entire ship and pier to hear, "*Now on the Ferrell, close all exterior doors. That is, close all exterior doors, now-now-now!*" He raged at the ensign, "*Post guards at all the mooring lines now-now-now!*"

This presented precisely the opportunity the rat needed. The quarterdeck watch, battered by these orders, failed to back up the petty officer of the watch who, facing the rat, had found himself frozen as he considered whether or not he had been specifically told to employ his sidearm. He drew and pointed the cold Colt model 1911a .45 caliber automatic, but the rat called his bluff and dived aboard.

Wyatt Earp

The truth is, the petty officer hadn't been bluffing at all. He actually pulled the trigger. But to his lifelong relief, the hammer fell with an empty click, which sounded like a door slamming shut to the messenger of the watch who found himself shocked into action by that little sound. The messenger, a very young sailor, whipped out his baton and proceeded to give chase as the rat scrambled down the main deck.

The petty officer placed his gun carefully back into its holster. Slowly at first, then with more enthusiasm, he followed the messenger. He had thought no one had seen him try to use his weapon, but the messenger of the watch and the three sailors waiting to go on liberty had all breathlessly awaited the gun's discharge, and had all felt disappointment in the petty officer's failure to achieve the Navy-wide level of mythic fame such an engagement would have given him if he had remembered to load the sidearm.

Later that afternoon, the petty officer of the watch would wonder why his shipmates kept chanting behind his back "Earp, Earp, Earp" as he tried to eat his dinner on the mess decks. He would discover that he'd earned the call sign "Wyatt Earp" which would follow him through the Navy, into college, and finally his law practice where it would achieve great utility when he became a truly deadly practitioner.

THAT'S WHAT XO'S DO

There has always been a sort of checklist normalcy to these raging moments when XOs clamp down to tighten up a ship that seems too loosely managed, and Ehrlich when he was XO of the Ferrell was no exception. There was Ehrlich's most sincerely enraged vilification of the department heads on the quarterdeck, especially when he caught two of them already in civilian khaki pants and polo shirts thereby visibly demonstrating the failure of purposeful oversight inherent to lackluster officers. There was Ehrlich's scatological description of the ship interspersed with threats of a perpetual field day of cleaning unless people started to do their jobs. There was the mustering of the master-at-arms force to bring nightsticks out for the sailors stationed to repel rats. There was the mustering of all hands at quarters for the department heads to give their permutation of the orders verbally nailed to their foreheads, and the subsequent scatter of sailors back to their berthing compartments to change out of their liberty clothes and back into their dungarees, scour every corner of the ship, clean everything over again and be ready for Ehrlich to storm through, holding up a dropped sock or candy wrapper as if it was flesh scourged from martyrs. "What's this! What's *this!* You call this fucking CLEAN?"

And most importantly, there was the ship-wide search for the rat guards.

That's what XO's do, and Ehrlich thought nothing of it. He would tour the ship enraged, spit commentary on every tiny shortcoming, let the crew know they were stuck together until they helped each other out. As far as he was concerned, they could all stay on board until they caught that rat, got up the rat guards, and by God DAMN, for once clean up this shithole! Why did he have to be the only one concerned about something like rat guards? It wasn't funny. Rats on board a ship are simply and literally pestilent. It's sloppy wrong and dangerous, and you can't afford that sort of shit, he bellowed—so. Shock all those tired sailors up onto their feet, in the engine room, the mess decks where they lolled in front of Italian TV—somebody had the motivation to rig that up. (No rat guards though. That would be too tough.) Snap them up out of their languor by a rush through the ship. No word even has to be said. His slam of a hatch alone would fully display all his pissed-off, XO rage at the crew who had already dropped the tight watch and careful habits they'd maintained at sea, dumped their responsibilities like the socks that littered the decks, and where were those rat guards anyway?

No one knew. Almost.

HIS ONLY HOPE

The rat guards had been stowed away by two sailors who had decided to get creative because the line-locker where they were normally kept had been filled with bicycles bought when the ship had visited Palma de Majorca two months before. However, of these two sailors, one had been medevaced—helicoptered off to the fancy sickbay on the aircraft carrier after he'd slipped down a ladder and broken his ankle.

And the other? Here was where coincidence played: one of the three sailors in their civvies who had thought they were going on liberty was a relatively senior boatswain's mate, Squiciarini, who was there at the front of the line because he had permission to go on leave to meet his wife's extended family who lived in Naples.

BM3 Squiciarini had actually given some consideration to telling Ops where the rat guards were placed. But he had decided to keep it to himself. He had thought his brain would burst if they didn't let him off the ship because he was sure he could see his wife's Italian relatives waiting for him at the distant gate to the pier, and he was pretty sure if he confessed to storing them fucking rat guards, he'd be the fuck back in his uniform, getting his ass chewed by the chief at least, and no fucking leave. Period. He had thought he was totally out of luck when the XO left his savage order to the quarterdeck: "Nobody leaves this ship until we catch that rat!"

With those words, the other two sailors about to go on liberty had slouched off, but in desperation, Squiciarini remained with his sea bag stuffed with civilian clothes and the cartons of cigarettes his wife's uncle would smoke for the next six months.

His only hope was Ops.

"Sir?"

Betrayal

What the operations officer saw was a boy still teenaged thin. Squiciarini's hair had already started to recede as it would until he paid for a weave when they finally got good at hair replacement the year before Ops was to have his what-the-fuck moment in the Pentagon. By then, long out of the Navy, Squiciarini would not know that Ops had been in the Pentagon. He will never know that Ops had become part of a memorial, and he will have long forgotten his sense of hopelessness as he looked at Ops, a twenty-seven-year-old officer with six years in the Navy whose perseverance had made him a lieutenant and a department head and therefore, in Squiciarini's world, an asshole. Probably a double asshole because he'd been grown in the Naval Academy in the years when the school's ethics code was generally known to be, "Don't lie, cheat or steal, but whatever you get away with is ok."

Ops had been a department head long enough to have a pretty good sense of what he could get away with, and it seemed to him a shame that poor Squiciarini, his relatives waiting for him, couldn't catch a break. Ops even thought that this small sailor standing limp before him, leave papers in his hand, might actually remember an act of kindness, and perhaps Ops would be known on the ship as one of those compassionate officers he'd always wished to become.

By now the messenger of the watch and Wyatt Earp had returned empty-handed to the quarterdeck, so there was an audience as Ops looked at the boy Squiciarini, thought of all the times he himself had wanted to be let off the hook. He held out his hand, "Give me your leave papers," and Squiciarini was certain these would be shoved in a drawer to be forgotten. His family would wait for him until they got tired, then leave, he was certain, but it wouldn't be his fault. It would be the ship's fault and the Navy's.

Ops took out his pen, signed him out on leave. "Squiciarini, I want you to hustle down the pier and don't let the XO see you standing around ashore, ok?"

That was *most* ok by Squiciarini and any lingering notion he had of telling anyone where those rat guards were stowed left him in the sense of urgency Ops had given him to leave the ship and escape recall by the XO.

Ops would never know anything about that betrayal. To him, it felt pretty good he had given a break to someone, and he could see the inconsequential ensign, the messenger, and Wyatt Earp look at him in wonder. He winked at them, feeling quite good about himself while the only person who knew where the rat guards had been stowed hustled guiltlessly down the brow and onto the pier to his reunion and great relief.

Ship's Lore and Shame

The way this should have come to an end: the rat guards should have finally been ferreted out after a short and organized search. Liberty would have been put down, and within the Naples bars that night, all the thousands of conversations between the one hundred sixty-eight officers, chief petty officers and sailors on liberty would have etched that day into memory as the Great Rat Hunt. It would have become a part of the ship's lore, fading slowly as each watch relieved each watch until the last person who remembered the Great Rat Hunt was gone, leaving the ship empty of anyone who had a personal stake in those words: "You think that was bad, you should have seen the Great Rat Hunt. One rat, and the XO kept us on board forever."

But the messenger of the watch changed all of that.

The messenger of the watch had the misfortune of birth as the oldest in a family of six children. He could not prevent the sure knowledge trained into him through his entire eighteen years of life that he should have done something to make sure the rat guards were up. He could not stand the discomfort of belonging to the one division on board the ship that had totally fucked up and was now the cause of the entire ship's incarceration on board and even worse, one of his division, that worthless Squiciarini, was already ashore. All his friends, those he admired, the ones who had taught him, praised and even looked after him—shamed. Even that. Still worse than a little ill-feeling, his witnessing of the ass-chewing the XO handed to Ops, then Ops' sticking his neck out to let Squiciarini off, who didn't deserve it—this shamed him. He could not resist thinking of Ops as the perfect big brother he'd never had. And that wink at him—it made him feel complicit, related, and well—*respected* was the word he wanted to find. Respected.

But he knew he didn't deserve any of that because he'd failed to kill the rat. After Squiciarini dragged his overstuffed sea bag onto the pier, he and Wyatt Earp had finally been able to make their report to Ops that the rat had slipped away. Ops had said, "Shit," rolled his eyes and he had said, "Christ, can't you guys to do anything right?"

Shame made the messenger decide to fix this, right away, on his own.

The American Practical Navigator

The messenger liked the ship, wandered it, knew its odd spaces. The flag bag trunk was the oddest space he could think of, a little closet where the signalmen kept their extra gear. Deep in the ship, hidden beneath four watertight hatches, the deepest destination of all those ladders down except the bilge, wet from condensation and slick with oil. The signalmen who owned the flag bag were air creatures, perched high in the ship to manipulate their semaphores and flags in the wind and the sun. They did not go below unless they needed parts for a broken halyard or a ripped signal flag.

He bet the rat guards were down there as, in fact, they were. They had been stowed in that bilge where there was a dry grating in an alcove above the bilge water pooled from all the condensation off the ship's hull. The messenger would get those rat guards, and the XO wouldn't be mad anymore, his chief would be proud of him, Ops would be rescued and consider him not only a hero, but perhaps his friend.

The messenger didn't tell anyone his plan and hoped no one else would figure it out. He had ambitions. He was pretty sure he wasn't quite like all the other guys in the deck force. He considered himself a little brighter and a little wiser. At sea, when on watch as the helmsman, he would frequently find himself chatting with the officers who were, after all, only a little older than himself. At work, he always did a bit more than was required of him. In port, once, he'd gotten a book to learn how to use small stuff to wrap handrails and helms with the intricate and turban-like knots called Turk's heads characteristic of particularly nautical and squared-away vessels. Everyone knew he kept a copy of Bowditch, the *American Practical Navigator* in his rack instead of the usual fuck book (not that he didn't have those also). But they didn't know he kept its quote in his wallet: "The officer whom the crew respects as a *man*, admires as a *seaman* and recognizes as a *gentleman* will have little or no trouble with discipline and cooperation of all on board."

RELIEVED

Finally, relieved of his watch and ignored by everyone, the messenger of the watch piped, "Permission to go below." No one answered; he edged away and ran to the ladder not down to the bilge, but up the seven decks to the small shack perched like a comic hat over the ship's pilothouse, the signal bridge. There, he found, as he expected, only the junior signalman, who had been posted, told to polish the space, then abandoned by his seniors to weather the XO's inspection alone.

"Give me the keys to the flag bag!" The messenger held out his hand. "I'll bet somebody threw the rat guards down in the bilge by the flag locker!"

The signalman wasn't supposed to hand up the keys, but he did it because he remembered some boatswain's mates had been down near the line locker one afternoon at sea and thought the messenger might be right. He even thought about closing up the signal shack and going with him, he was so sure of it, but the leading signalman had ordered him under no circumstances to be gone when the XO made it up to the signal shack to inspect its corners and crannies. The signalman gave the messenger the keys and stayed where he was supposed to stay, which was a good thing or there would have been two of them.

Guardian

Of all his travels through the ship, the messenger loved the skip down the ladders from the signal bridge to the lower decks the best. He had done this many, many times, even in his one year on board. It always meant he was going off watch, flying down free and light after relief from the pilothouse or as lookout, the path through the ship which seemed to presage the future he imagined for himself as he twirled through the empty pilothouse where he could envision himself, most certainly, standing watch as the officer of the deck underway, guardian of all on board, the movement and safety of the ship at sea, then below, past the combat information center, where he was certain he would one day rule as the tactical action officer, fighting the ship, exercising gun and missile, past the captain's in-port cabin, a palace he dared desire in his secret wishes known to all. He evaded officers' country and the wardroom, where one day he would eat with all his brother officers, stiff-walked forward ("Never run on the ship," XO says) then down another hatch past the chief's mess where, he imagined, one day his loyal chief would guide the good men of his division, and past the hatch down to the chief engineer's main control, that unknown realm of engines and fuel and water he was certain he could master—until he came to the big lower deck hatch to the trunk, big enough to allow the hoist of a refrigerator-sized pump when opened. The hatch was bolted heavily down, its gasket dogged onto a coaming by eight fat nuts. In its center, a small circular hatch called a scuttle gave access for a single person at a time with a quick-acting wheel to spin it loose.

He stopped. He unlocked the scuttle. He would only be down there for a minute. He spun the wheel to loosen the dogs and it popped up. He stepped through with the trick of stepping forward, down onto the ladder. He slipped in and hesitated for an instant before closing it after him. Someone might see and ask some question to stop him. Someone would check on an opened scuttle, and he knew he wasn't supposed to be down this hatch. This was a hatch they locked closed for some reason.

Shipmates

It was a strange piece of luck for Ehrlich to find the scuttle. Some might say there was some invisible hand at work in this, but there wasn't. He was only doing his job.

Ehrlich thought, *This is what the XO does, this is what the XO does, he squares it away, he squares it away,* as he hustled down the passageway to get to the engineers' berthing compartment where he knew it was going to be an absolute disaster. He'd come from the chief's mess where he had encountered the command master chief and two of his cronies having coffee. The master chief's pals, he told *them* to get out in their spaces and be ready to present them for inspection or he would fail them on the spot. They lazily emptied out their cups, rinsed them, left him alone with the master chief to whom the XO said, "I'd think you'd be out helping the crew get off on liberty, Master Chief."

The command master chief did not have a division; his purpose was the running of the chief's mess and the support of the crew. Ehrlich thought of him as a union boss, but by regulation, he was the captain's direct advisor, the senior enlisted man on board. That position, plus his age, nearing fifty and his retirement that loomed with bewildering proximity only three months away, let him say, "The crew's liberty? I'd say that's your lookout now, Shipmate."

This is where the word 'shipmate' becomes derogatory, scathing and belittling. In such a little sentence, the senior enlisted man on the ship, older than Ehrlich but no wiser, perfectly communicated insubordination in a manner that could not be punished—they were alone—with these few words, he expressed his contempt for Ehrlich's rampage, threatened to describe all to the captain upon his return, and imparted his estimation that Ehrlich had failed in every respect as a *man*, a *seaman*, and a *gentleman*.

Ehrlich walked out of the chief's mess without a word, knowing all of it true.

The Scuttle

Ehrlich was no longer enraged when he saw the scuttle, closed but only partially dogged down, the padlock loose on the lid. He chanted to himself, "This is what the XO does, this is what the XO does."

A better man would have simply found the rat guards.

Put them up.

Gotten rat guards from somewhere else.

"He squares it away. He squares it away. This is what the XO does."

Maybe he had a right.

A better man would have simply fixed the problem instead of this ringing out, this endorsement of terror. Foolish to act like this. But the crew, so stupid and dangerous leaving a hatch like that unlocked. He opened the hatch, looked down. Empty.

Sloth. He'd let his ship go to sloth. Ehrlich knew, then, that he hadn't been as diligent as he ought to have been.

He'd been too slack.

Ehrlich dogged the hatch down, locked it. He stalked away to the quarterdeck to see if anyone could find some way to come up with new rat guards.

REPOSED

The ship had been waiting for someone. The long, deep trunk into the flag locker and bilge, through every deck, lower and lower. Doors on each level led to compartments, locked and secured, watertight, airtight; their rubber gaskets pressed onto their knife edges to seal pump rooms, electronic spaces, storage rooms—sealing them shut against the danger of flood and fire—these empty spaces of the ship had been waiting for someone. Brightly lit, the trunk invited the messenger down one ladder then the next, and further even five decks below to the bottom where the messenger tried his keys on the flag locker. Of course, now he couldn't remember why he thought that the rat guards would be in the flag locker; the signalmen would never store anything for the boatswain's mates, it was all too confusing to work out, his judgment already affected by the deep breaths of methane he'd taken going down the vertical ladders, step-by-step, breathing it in where it had seeped up over time from potatoes dropped months before from the bag a working party had broken on the edge of the opened hatch as they filled the ship's stores. Six potatoes, left in the bilge water to fester. Later, other sailors in another compartment deep in the trunk installed new stanchions in place to mount equipment, and they had left behind the inert gas used by their arc welder, argon. Heavier than air, the argon had settled into the bilge over time and shouldered aside some of the oxygen the messenger might have found to prevent ship's methane from working so quickly.

He tried the keys on the flag locker's padlock, in a hurry because the ship had given him a nagging sense that he might be late for something, confused even further by the carbon dioxide pooled in the bottom of the trunk from the fire extinguisher once used to put out the trash basket fire caused by a spatter of welding slag. There was something he was supposed to do, something he had to do for the operations officer. It had to do with the bilge and for a moment, he remembered the missing rat guards and remembered he'd seen them in the bilge. (He had not. He had only imagined them so.) He dropped the keys on the deck, stepped down the short ladder into the bilge where it was dark. Quiet in there. So quiet. No ventilation, no creaks or ticks. The ship stationary next to the pier, not even the mumble of the ship's propulsion. But this made no difference to the ship's wet rust. It slipped under the bubbled paint of the I-beams of the ship's framing, squirmed under his feet. Someone called out. No matter. He had his sea legs and maintained his balance. He did not slip into the five inches of water with the moldy scum on top exuding a slight scent of rotten eggs, the hydrogen sulfide's contribution to the carbon dioxide and now, even carbon monoxide trapped under the low overhead of the deck above the bilge.

The messenger couldn't remember why he was there, then remembered he was supposed to bring something, but what? He had done something wrong. He shouldn't be in the bilge. He climbed back up the four ladder rungs into the light. But he was so tired. His arms didn't seem attached. He was supposed to take his arms back up to the top of the trunk, but they were too heavy, so he sat down. He'd been up very, very early that morning; he'd risen up through the ship with the promising scent of the night baking all around him and out into the clean air of the sea breeze wafting ashore from the first limbs of the rising sun. He had gone on watch to come into port and after arrival—he had been on watch and that had been enough done in one day, as his father used to tell him, enough done to take a break. He leaned back against the door of the flag locker to close his eyes. The quiet whisper of the hold descended upon him like the warm hand of his mother grateful to him for all his younger brothers, sound and home, grateful for all his duty performed. And he—most grateful for this quiet moment in the vast hollow under all decks, low, alone, reposed.

POINTED FAIR

THEY HAD US PARKED directly under the bay bridge in that godless shipyard, not even as good as a bicycle shop. They get you in the dock for a week—purgatory while they find equipment your crew had gotten used to seeing broken. Next thing, the commodore chews your ass for the extra three million they had not expected to spend on you, now it's four million, now six. One repair finds another, bad wiring, broken piping. Once they even found a silver dollar stood on edge in a steel trough welded by some yard bird onto a rib under the XO's cabin. Shipyard workers, how richly they deserved to be called *yard birds* in their fat, filthy coveralls and nasty attitudes. They wouldn't last a year in the Navy, yard birds leaving behind nasty jokes even when they aren't hammering off old paint with such delight. That howling, premeditated roar, especially inside the ship under the little flight deck where the grinders batter off the non-skid, epoxy paint used to grip the tires of the helicopter we had carried at sea, the grinders with chainsaw teeth screaming against the steel.

I told the command master chief, "Make sure everyone has good hearing protection."

He couldn't hear me over the noise. "What?"

"Hearing Protection! Hearing Protection for Everyone!"

The master chief laughed, stuck up a thumb. "Done. Already done."

Of course, it was already done. The first day in dock, I'd come aboard ship to see the master chief at the quarterdeck, watching. Unusual. I asked him how come he'd decided to watch the crew come aboard and he said, "I don't like that long brow from the edge of the drydock. Remember that drydock in Brooklyn, that graving dock?"

When had I been a lieutenant? How long ago? Twenty years—the command master chief and I had served together on one of the old single screw steam frigates. Both of us young and dumb, we'd expected the Navy to be nothing but open seas, gunnery and distant ports on a sleek ship pointed fair. Neither of us had imagined we'd be trapped for weeks under the thumbs of yard birds, but there we were again. Both of us old. Me in command, the master chief my senior enlisted advisor, both of us shipmates again. Maybe it was luck, maybe fate we would both end our sea-going careers where we had started, dry on the hard in dock.

Of course, this San Diego version of a dock was a far cry from that Brooklyn antique. Vintage Civil War, they'd dug a massive pit, lined it with stone blocks and pumped water out of the basin to lower a century of ships deep onto wooden blocks set on the floor of a canyon, great doors keeping out the turd-strewn Brooklyn waters—a graving dock, shaped like a grave, our little frigate riding tiny inside, impossibly high and bare above its floor.

A sailor, drunk from some Manhattan night, had started to cross the brow in the wee-hours of the midwatch. Somehow, he slipped through the railings, fluttered through and was gone. The master chief and I had seen the boy's last living movement, the insentient stretching of his limbs like a bug crushed underfoot.

We were different from those days, the master chief and I. He'd gotten thicker in the limbs, slower in speech, darker around the eyes. The bristle of his crew cut, thinner, greyer. I'd lost most any hair I had and a fair part of my sight, but we felt pretty much the same, I reckon, as we did when we were boys. He watched the crew come up onto our fancy west coast brow and told me, "Crew hates coming back to work so much they don't pay enough attention. Or they're still half shitfaced. I keep my eye out. I make sure the railings are well woven with line. A rat couldn't fall off our brow, Captain. But a sailor might find a way."

This was the sort of man who made sure everyone's hearing was protected before I could think of it. This was the sort of man who made the first part of the day fine for me, seeing each other every morning and comparing notes even if we had to holler over the noise. A rare thing anywhere, even in the Navy—an old friend, a shipmate from years before, ten minutes of shared coffee and understanding even after the yard birds fire up their machines and you stuff the yellow earplugs in, take an aspirin, pray for the day to end.

That howl, four hours every morning, one-hour lunch break, three and one-half hours in the afternoon, knock off on the instant, so no one pays overtime. Yard birds taking it out on the ship as if they were actually beating your skull over and over until that day when it stopped, a shocking silence at a little after three that afternoon.

At first, I was relieved. Who wouldn't be happy for a little peace? Then I take a look at the clock, and I see they'd quit twenty minutes early. I first think they're done. But not yet. We had another week to go. The yard birds must have broken something, or maybe we did. I imagined their complaint about us, interference owing to some evolution of the crew, say a fire drill, or one of my sailors moving equipment through their work areas. Anything would do to give this stinking bicycle shop an excuse to knock off early, extend the work another day or two. Twenty minutes here, twenty minutes there, and everyone makes out. Overtime for the yard birds, another day on the contract for the drydock, another two dozen man-days of chargeable expense for the contractor, and what's another twenty-eight thousand dollars to the government? Stopping early like that fired me up and I was all ready to flame spray somebody when my desk phone rings. It sounded so strange in the silence.

Maybe I snapped at her. "What?"

I regret it. She was one of my sharper young lieutenants, Olivia Luce, on duty. She'd been with us at sea and I could sleep when Olivia had been on watch. She was the kind of lieutenant I hope I had been, but she had started her report with that uncertain voice they get when you answer the phone pissed off. "Captain, sir, the Coast Guard told the shipyard there was somebody up on the highway, on the bridge."

I remember what that's like, trying to anticipate an angry captain's question. And I could have said something like, "So what? Why do we care?" But I had learned to wait, quietly, for my lieutenants to find their words. You have to let them get it out and she did, finally. "I guess it's a girl or something, trying to jump, Captain. They said—she might jump. So the shipyard knocked off work."

"Where?" I asked her.

"Everywhere, sir. The whole shipyard knocked off."

"No, Lieutenant. Where's the jumper?"

"Somewhere on the bridge."

"Over us?"

"Uhh."

Routine, tradition, procedure—those we have in the Navy. But Lieutenant Luce had been caught in a strange place, making a report to her captain that was outside all that normal routine, tradition or procedure. I told her I'd be on the foc'sle. Then I added, "Near the bow," so she would remember what I said while she was wondering if the jumper would land on our ship.

Things fall on a ship in drydock. You wear a hard hat, always. People leave tools aloft in the masts. Even a tiny bolt or nut kicked loose will cave in a skull. Sometimes a stone or some road accident crap will drop from the bridge onto the ship, just enough to make it possible to ruin your day with an injury, even with the hard hat on. But no one expects anyone to jump onto the ship. Maybe I should have told my lieutenant that they always jump for the bay.

By the time I got outside, the yard birds had dropped their tools and wandered out to the edge of the pier next to the drydock, smoking and hanging around, waiting. My crew had started to come out to the weather decks, no noise, the air quiet, they'd gathered at the lifelines and upper decks, the word had spread through the ship like the odor you get when some vandal breaks a sewage line.

I was about to start telling people to get back inside, but the command master chief had already burst out on deck to run off all the Lookie-Loos. He cleared them off, got me to tell the XO to put down early liberty to let those not on watch go home. All I had to do was call the shipyard and shit on the safety officer until he agreed to have security send the labor force away. When we finished our work, the master chief and I found ourselves alone together at the point of the bow.

These modern, west coast docks are marvels. Floating steel, they lift eight thousand tons as if it were air, and our ship rode high as an altar above the bay where we could look out over the sill of the drydock to the clean surface beyond. Three harbor police and Coast Guard small craft lolled around on the glassy water in the shadow of the bridge. No wind. No traffic sounds. Everything seemed calm. We couldn't see anything. Only the boats marking the spot where she would fall.

The master chief gave me that particular salute of his, a little slower, not a snap. A lift of a careful hand. "Captain," he said.

"Command Master Chief." I lifted my own hand, dropped it. We had not planned to meet on the foc'sle. But we both knew where we would find each other, and we both knew he would tell me, "If they wait, they doan do it. You oughta go back inside. You go on inside, Captain. I'll make sure nobody comes back out on deck except me. I'll keep an eye."

You want to believe in wisdom from a guy like the master chief. But it seemed like a failure of responsibility, somehow important that I, the commanding officer, should stay out on watch, just the same way it had seemed important to get rid of the curious, give this poor girl some dignity, whether or not she let herself go. It felt like I was doing something, as if somehow being in command, I could affect some outcome.

What a joke.

Thirty years in the Navy, I should have known more about command, especially in dock. Navy Regulations state, when the ship's stem crosses the sill of the drydock, the docking officer owns the responsibility for her movement. The captain has no command of anything until "...the extremity of the ship last to leave the dock clears the sill and the ship is pointed fair..."

But does a captain ever really have command? The ship does not really belong to any commander, does it? You may be the ship's captain, but I believe in my heart of hearts, it is never the captain's ship. It is our ship.

What had really happened?

I had only cleared the decks after the master chief had pointed out what a problem it would be if there was a picture, *Crew of Navy Destroyer Watches Suicide.* Never be the headline. That's always good advice.

It was a long fall.

By chance, we were staring at the exact point where she went. The master chief jerked his hands out as if trying to catch hers. "Holy Christ, look." She hit the water a breath after he got it out. She accelerated to the end. It was not as if she started slow. She had started with a drop, but she sped up. She was well away from the ship, a dark form between us and the low afternoon sun.

Imagine someone on her way home. She stops the car, gets out. She must have stood there for about a half hour. People must have tried to talk her out of it. But she let herself over the edge, let go.

Not much splash even. She had seemed rigid. An arm, or leg, something had stuck out at the instant before she hit.

That's all we saw, really. We would never know. We saw that dark plunge and the arm or something.

The master chief whispered, "Oh, Captain—oh, Captain. I didn't need to see that."

"The poor, poor girl," I said. "Somebody's poor baby."

The master chief stepped toward me. "Captain." He gripped my elbow. "Didn't you see? " He stood as still as a rock, stared at me until I stepped away. "That was no girl who fell, no woman."

"They said it was a woman. Lieutenant Luce said it was a girl trying to jump."

"Trying to jump." Full of wonder, the master chief looked back to the water. "Captain. That was no girl."

Sometimes you do things, you don't know why. I found Lieutenant Luce cocooned alone deep inside the ship at the wardroom table where we officers take our meals. She had poured a cup of coffee, and I suppose the cook had given her a wafer cookie on a plate where it rested, untouched. She bolted up and said, "Attention on Deck!" as if I was entering a room with a crowd.

Luce was not a small person. And you got the sense of firm shoulders already accustomed to bearing the weight. "At ease," I said, as if I was about to deliver all the answers. As if I could. All I could do is sit across the table from her and tell her, "Olivia, the person jumped."

"Did you see it, captain?"

"Master chief says it was a man. Did you see it?"

She flinched. "I watched from the pilothouse."

"Was it a man?"

She looked away into the distance, and I remembered how it felt the first time I saw death, how my whole life had compressed inside that obscene silence, and she said, "What difference does it make?"

What difference?

Did she wonder what the dead thought in their last moments falling through the still air over the clean bay? Did she wonder who we become, we who watch in the same air, sweet and smooth, all of us seeing clear across the water, seeing people come out onto the park to look at the bridge reflected on the glassy, wetter ground? Did my lieutenant ask herself what we have done, what we have failed to do? Did she hear the air rush past when she was still pointed so fair?

ACKNOWLEDGEMENTS

I owe a world of thanks to so many who will always remain close to my heart.

Every gratitude to Ruth Thompson and Don Mitchell, who plucked me from an author's bio to risk publishing this book at Saddle Road Press, and to splendid Henry Thayer, who never seems to lose his confidence in my work no matter the world's response.

A powerful thanks to the Bread Loaf and Sewanee Writers' Conferences, and to the Warren Wilson MFA Program for Writers who gave me the sharpest tools of the craft and an even more important sense of belonging to a great venture.

My deepest gratitude to the Camargo Institute where Bread Loaf funded me on a Bakeless fellowship, to MacDowell Colony, and to the Virginia Center for the Creative Arts. These stories could not have been written without the gifts of their community, time and encouragement.

To my friends, teachers and wonderful readers, I am ever grateful: Jeremy Bass, Andrea Barrett, Jen Calder, Robert Cohen, Peter Ho Davis, Stephen Dobyns, Kim Frank, Goldie Goldbloom, Elizabeth Gray Jr., David Haynes, Geoff Kronik, Kevin McIlvoy, Alexander Parsons, Jane Porter, C.E. Poverman, Pete Turchi, Steve Wingate, Brent Walth, and my editor of all things, Christopher Shelton.

To the literary hero of my lifetime, Tim O'Brien, who gave me the turn that made the story "Prerogatives." To Professors Max Zimmer, Hal Moore and David Kranes, University of Utah, who bequeathed a lifetime of joy when they encouraged a twenty-four-year-old sailor to tell stories. To Heather McHugh who convinced a passed-over, retired naval officer that his stories were worth telling.

And to Captain Sharon Shelton, United States Navy, (retired), who is my beacon, my navigator, and my ever-constant clear eye on the horizon.

ABOUT THE AUTHOR

Rolf Yngve enlisted in the United States Navy as a seaman in 1971 and retired from active duty as a captain in 2006 after thirteen deployments on nine ships and sea going staffs. He commanded *USS Oldendorf (DD-982)* from 1996 to 1998. His short fiction has been published in a number of journals and anthologies including *Best American Short Stories, 1979*. He earned an MFA from the Warren Wilson MFA for Writers program in 2012 and lives in Coronado, California with his spouse, Captain Sharon Shelton, USN (retired).

CPSIA information can be obtained
at www.ICGtesting.com
Printed in the USA
FFHW021623150219
50537107-55835FF